PREY

THE UNMASKED SERIES #1

For all you good girls (and boys) who crave a night with four

masked men...

Content Warning

This is the first book in a six part (including this one) dark romance why-choose series. All the characters are between the ages of 25 and 35.

Within these pages and between the characters, many things happen. This is a dark MMMFFM romance with multiple POV. If that's not your thing, that's okay, but then this book isn't for you.

Please note that while I list the warnings for this particular book, the themes will grow darker as the series moves forward. If you can stomach the idea that these characters will endure far more than what's written (typed) on these pages, then please proceed.

THEMES:

Dark, mafia, friends to lovers, bi-awakening, why-choose

CONTENT:

Detailed graphic sexual content including *extremely* thorough scenes with two-, three-, and four-person sexual encounters that include things such as choking/breath play, degradation, praise, dom/sub, biting, cream pie cleanup, exhibitionism, and voyeurism.

Bi-Awakening

Violence and weapons

People are un-alived on page

Kidnapping and bondage

Mention of forced sexual situations and violence (not on page)

If you're still here...

Enjoy.

Playlist

River - BRKN LOVE

Trapped in a Dream - Rudy Wade

Taste - Stray Kids

Way Down We Go - Kaleo

Sex on Fire - Kings of Leon

One of the Girls - The Weekend/Lily Rose Depp

Intoxicated - Aaryan Shah

American Horror Show - Snow Wife

FMLYHM - Seether

Like You Mean It - Steven Rodriguez

Who's a Good Girl - Manic Kazzy

Gangsta - Kehlani

Animal - Jim Yosef/RIELL

Something in Your Mouth - Nickleback

Beg - Aryia

Tainted Love - Marilyn Manson

Desire - Meg Myers

All I Want - Cameron Grey

Bad Moon Rising - Credence Clearwater Revival

Not All Men - Morgan St. Jean

Numb - Tommee Profitt/Skylar Grey

Saints - Echos

The Emptiness Machine - Linkin Park

Let the World Burn - Chris Grey

Insane - Black GryphOn, Baasik

Joke's On You - Charlotte Lawrence

CHAPTER 1

DELILAH

O F ALL THE TIMES to forget my wallet, tonight is the worst.

"You don't need your wallet, Delilah," Cora says to me, tossing her fiery red hair over her shoulder, and winks at the bartender, slipping him her card. A flirty smile curves her lip as she grazes her fingers over the back of his hand. "Keep the tab open."

"My entire life is in that wallet," I tell my friend, a wave of irritation rushing through me that I allowed Cora to drag me here in the first place.

The bartender's gaze darts to me. Recognition flashes across his face, his eyes widening in fear for a fraction of a second before composing himself. He slides her card back across the black, glossy bar top, smiling with forced enthusiasm. "Drinks are on the house, ladies."

With a wink, Cora picks up her card and slips it back into the little wristlet strung around her forearm. Turning back to me, she cocks her head to the side, eyebrows going up. "See?" She smirks. "You don't even need your wallet. Just your face."

Yeah. Except maybe sometimes I just want *not* to be recognized. To move through life undetected. Faceless. Nameless. Invisible. Safe from expectations and judgment.

Sometimes, being Rune Gavin's daughter is more a curse than anything.

Especially when you're trying to slip quietly through his club.

I ignore my best-friend's knowing gaze, averting my eyes to scan the busy space. The dimly lit main floor is drenched in a garish blue glow. Long beams of rosy pink laser lights flash overhead, skittering over the shifting bodies crowding the floor, decked in various costumes. Music thumps like a heartbeat, reverberating through my body in time with the lights, making my heart feel like it's pumping with the same beat.

The club is alive, pulsating with the loud music, filled with people seeking a night of pleasure and mischief. That's part of why I didn't want to attend tonight's event. Too many people and too much...

Everything.

The other reason is probably up in one of the hotel's rooms, getting his dick sucked by his secretary. Again.

The hairs on the back of my neck stand on end, a strange needling sensation sliding down my arms like someone's dragging long claws over my flesh. My gaze is drawn to the back of the club where the VIP lounge is located. Several plush couches create U-shaped seating areas and in the center, I catch sight of a skull mask before the press of bodies moving through the club block it from view.

The elbow of the girl next to me hits my lower back and I shift more towards Cora to make space for her to order her drinks, trying not to let her obvious rudeness bother me.

The day, hell, the entire *week,* has worn on me. Numbers and contracts run through my head, a kaleidoscope of greed. I need to let go of the stressful meeting I was forced to attend this morning with the arrogant man who made me want to spit fire in his direction. When I close my eyes, I can still see his sunglasses looking back at me from the video monitor. The asshole didn't even have the decency to attend in person, instead connecting via video call.

Cora's hand lands on my arm, jolting me back. Her eyes slide down to my legs and she quirks a brow. "Besides, where would you even put your wallet?" she asks, leaning forward to grab our drinks as the bartender slides them over. "You're not wearing any pants, Delly-belly. "

"My wallet has a strap like yours," I remind her, rolling my eyes at her nickname for me and carefully take my drink, the dark liquid spilling over the top as the girl behind me jostles me yet again.

My teeth gnash together as the girl's elbow digs into my back. I bite back an angry retort and force my way through the people gathered around the bar. Cora grabs my shoulder from behind and I lead us away from the bar and further into the club. We are forced to stop when the buckle of a man's long leather jacket catches on my fishnets and we have to stop to untangle ourselves before we move forward.

Cora better thank me later. But I'd do anything for her, and she knows it. Including come to my father's club when it's the last place I want to be.

Glancing up to the upper level, my shoulders sag. People lean over the railing, peering down at the dance floor, taking up nearly every inch of space. We're definitely not going up there. I survey the large club, my sights settling for a moment on the back where I know we could easily get a spot in the VIP lounge. Flashing a pretty smile at a bouncer would secure us a place for people watching.

No. That's one thing I hate doing. Using Rune's power to get what I want.

We stop next to a group of young women who look barely old enough to be here, much less shooting back the rows of shots lined up on the table before them. I look down at my costume, wondering if I made a wrong choice tonight. The girls next to us all match, wearing skimpy Playboy bunny outfits, bunny ears, and flashy heels. Frowning, I skim my free hand over my ass, regretting my costume choice.

Cora convinced me to dress up and come to this costume party, even though I really wanted to spend tonight tucked in my bed with a pint of ice cream and a sappy Netflix movie, continuing to lick my wounds. But no. According to my best friend, I'm too young to act this old.

I say I'm too young to have been married, cheated on, and divorced, but such is life.

"Fuck it," Cora says loudly, holding up her drink for a toast. "Tonight is for fun and debauchery!"

A wave of intense excitement, tangled with a dark nervousness, twists in my gut. I want to enjoy the night, the temptation to say, "fuck it," nearly consuming, but...

But nothing. For years I've told myself I'm going to let loose. Be more like Cora. Not let my father rule every decision I make. Tonight is as good as any. I raise my glass with a determined smile, clinking our drinks together. "Fuck it."

We both down our drinks and I wince at the strong liquor as it burns a hot path down my throat and settles in my belly.

"God, girl, you look so hot." Cora leans in, her eyes sparkling as she takes in my black fishnet stockings and knee-high boots. "Sexy little Catwoman."

I glance down at my outfit. She wanted to dress as villains, so I opted for Catwoman since that's the only costume I could come up with that didn't require me leaving my condo to purchase anything new on such short notice, apart from my mask with cat ears I saw in a boutique yesterday. I had found the black stretchy bodysuit in my closet from my sexy witch costume years ago, and decided it would have to do. What seemed like a good idea an hour ago now has me pants-less in a crowded club. And without my wallet, because I forgot the damn thing when Cora rushed me out of my house. I only have my phone tucked in my bra for safekeeping thanks to the fact I was holding it when she shoved me out the door and into the taxi.

Shooting her a scowl, I brush my wild locks from my face as I take in her outfit. I left my hair loose, the black waves falling down my back. Besides the black winged-eyeliner barely visible under my little mask, I have no makeup on. Cora has garish green eye shadow and bright red lips. She went with Poison Ivy, a perfect costume for my red-haired friend, after she found a shiny green leotard in a vintage boutique last week. At least I'm not the only one not wearing pants.

My eyes drift back to the young girls, the group laughing and throwing back shots. They aren't wearing pants either.

Fuck it, right? It is, after all, Halloween. The one night a year where pants at social events are optional.

"Damn, girl," a male voice says behind us, making both Cora and I turn at the same time.

Freddy Kruger, red striped sweater and all, stands holding a drink, the loose-fitting mask obscuring his face. The guy is disregarding the club's ban on full face masks. Hell, half of those in attendance aren't abiding by the club rule. I've seen several Jason masks and one Michael Myers since we arrived.

"That ass is delicious," Freddy says, and I instinctively place my drink-free hand on my rear end.

"Thanks." Cora flashes him a smile, her gaze flickering down his tall frame and back up to his masked face. The black eyes give me a creepy feeling, as if they are focused solely on me. "Her tits are amazing, too."

The second I see her flirty eyes and her classic lip bite, dread pools in my belly. We made a deal before we even stepped foot in this place that we'd leave together. No splitting up. No going home with strange men. Yet, the very first man to talk to us and she's ready to strip her shiny green leotard off and sit on this guy's lap.

"So I see," Freddy says, making my skin crawl.

She gestures to his mask. "You want to play a game?"

Freddy gives a light shrug. "Sure."

Cora cocks a brow, sipping her drink. "Don't you want to know what the game is before you agree to it?"

"What's the game?" he asks dutifully, pulling his mask away from his face so he can slip the straw of his drink underneath.

A sly smile spreads over her bright red lips. Tucking an unruly curl behind her ear, she leans forward. Freddy leans closer, his mask's evil smirk and flat eyes locked onto me. Not even shifting to the right helps. They seem to follow me.

"If I guess the color of your eyes, you buy us a drink," she says.

Freddy leans back on his heels, setting his drink on a nearby table. "And if you're wrong? What do I get?"

Biting her lip, Cora asks, "What do you want?"

Resisting the urge to roll my eyes, I set my drink down next to his and cross my arms over my chest, feeling exposed by the way he's looking at me. I know my tits and ass are hanging out, and usually, I'm a confident person. I have to be even when I'm not, but this guy is giving me the creeps, making me want to cover up and scurry away.

"He wants your number," I inform her. They always, always ask for a number. My little five-foot-four friend is beautiful.

Then again, Cora's changed this game tonight. She usually says we'll guess his name, which seems to stack the odds against us, but the point of the game is to get it wrong, so she's forced to give him her number.

"Maybe I want yours," Freddy says, scooting in closer to me, filling my nose with the sweet smell of cheap cologne. His head shifts slightly toward Cora. "Maybe I want both of yours."

Cora lets out a loud laugh. "Kinky, Kruger. I like it."

"How about, instead of your number..." Freddy tilts his head side to side like he's thinking and I'm bored with this conversation already. "If you guess wrong, I get a kiss from both of you."

Oh, now that's a new one.

"Bold." Cora gestures at his mask. "You're assuming we'd want to kiss the face hidden under there?"

"Actually," a deep masculine voice says from my right, making me jolt sideways. My arms drop, but I keep one hand pressed over my thumping heart as I turn to see who snuck up on me.

My eyes land on a wall of muscle. Lots of muscles. A large hulking figure stands next to me. His broad chest is wrapped in a tight black long sleeve shirt, straining against bulging biceps crossed over his chest, his gloved hands gripping thick forearms. My gaze dips to a pair of black fatigues, hugging massive thighs, the pants hem tucked into black combat boots. I tilt my head and step backward to take him all in.

When my eyes meet his, my mouth goes dry.

CHAPTER 2

DELILAH

ONLY HIS EERILY PALE eyes are visible, surrounded by dark skin, shadowed by heavy black brows, and framed with long black eyelashes. His eyes may be blue, but it's hard to tell with how dark the club is, making them seem colorless like ice. The rest of his face is hidden behind a skull ski mask covering his entire head, gathering loosely around his neck, leaving cutouts for his striking eyes. He's so tall that I take another step back to see him fully, snapping my jaw closed. He's dressed like a video game character on a reconnaissance mission to save the world.

"This game is over," he says, those pale eyes on Freddy, a dangerous glint sparking in them.

"Why don't you fuck off, buddy?" Freddy crosses his arms over this chest. Even though he's just as tall as Recon, he's nowhere near as big, so getting mouthy seems like a bad idea on his part.

Before I can blink, Recon's arm shoots out, and he grips Freddy by the neck with a massive gloved hand. "How about you leave these girls alone?" he growls. "Buddy."

"Shit man," Freddy gasps. "No need to get nuts. We're just having some fun."

Freddy grips the massive hand around his neck, trying to break free, but Recon shakes him as he drags him closer.

"Was that your plan?" Recon asks with such menace in his voice, the words scraping across my skin, each syllable running a chill down my arms. "Have some *fun* with these girls?"

Freddy opens his mouth to respond, but Recon's gloved hand clamps down like a vise, trapping the words in his throat.

"I recognize men like you." Recon's eyes blaze with fury as he leans in close to Freddy, emphasizing each word until they feel like a physical threat. "You're a fucking predator."

"Hey, Recon." I step closer, placing a hand on his arm, desperation flooding me. My eyes sweep the club, looking for one of the club's bouncers, or worse, one of my father's guards, and I send a silent prayer that no one's paying attention. The last thing I want is Rune alerted that I'm in the club causing problems. "I appreciate your overly aggressive protection, but you can let him go."

His angry, light eyes travel down, locking onto the hand I've positioned on his bicep. I squeeze it a bit to emphasize my words, feeling the unmistakable raw power he emanates under my palm.

Recon's grip loosens, and he shoves Freddy back, sending him stumbling into the table with the Bunny's. Freddy grunts as his back hits the table and the girl's all cry out, pushing him away as they try to save their spilled drinks.

"Fuckin' whatever, man," Freddy says, tugging at his shirt and adjusting his mask. He gestures to me. "You can have that ass. It's not worth it."

"Oh, it's worth it," Recon snaps. He turns slightly and points behind him. We all step sideways to look around his massive bulk. In the dim VIP area of the club, a man wearing a similar recon costume sits with two others in matching uniforms, their skull masks illuminated under the blue light, gashes of pink neon flashing across them. "But it belongs to him."

"Excuse me?" I hiss, my eyes widening as I rip my gaze from the men sitting on the plush couches, to glare at Recon as Freddy slinks away.

Cora lets out a strangled sound. I glance at her, but she's watching the three men in the VIP lounge like they're the only ones left in the entire club.

"Reaper told me to escort you to him." Recon extends an arm in a silent command, telling me to lead the way. "Now."

"Is that so?" I lift a brow, my eyes gravitating back to the three.

The one in the middle looks bigger than the two men at his sides, but it may just be the way he's sitting. Legs spread out carelessly, arms thrown over the back of the couch. He seems to consume the air in the room, leaving nothing for the rest of us. A giant god among mere mortals, commanding attention, and we're all revolving around him, here to please him.

"After you." Recon gestures again, but this time, he places his other hand on my lower back. A jolt of lightning sends a shock of awareness through me. My nipples tighten at the sensation of his large hand pressing into my back, and I sidestep his touch, not liking how my body responds to this stranger. Aware that my very first instinct was to obey.

Breaths a little too quick, I meet Recon's pale eyes. "And who is Reaper?"

"You'll find out when you go, won't you, Tiny Thing?"

A sudden, burning urge to march over and demand why this Reaper guy thinks he can command me pierces through my gut and I straighten my spine, glaring across the club like I can see him even though layers of people block him from my view.

Recon's hand presses against my lower back again and that same awareness floods my core, but I don't step back. The sensation sits there, warm and heavy, until I realize it feels faintly like arousal. His simple touch, his presence and his soft demand, is turning me on. Maybe even a little of the mystery of who he is. Who they are.

He lowers his masked mouth to my ear and says, "Reaper doesn't like to be left waiting."

Balling my hands into fists, I lift my chin, taking a determined step forward, but still when I feel Cora's hand land on my arm.

"We're doing this?" she asks, brows knit as she steps beside me. A flash of disbelief crashes through me. Cora, my crazy, risk-taking friend, is being cautious? Now? She eyes Recon and looks back at me. "You sure?"

My eyes dart between her and this large man in the VIP lounge, demanding my presence. With a shrug, I say, "Fuck it, right?"

The corner of her red lips quirk, a sly smirk taking over, washing away her nervous expression.

With Recon at our back, my eyes on the three men, I stalk across the club, a rushing energy tingling through my veins. My heart skitters in my chest, harder and faster than the music, but I can only hear the *thump, thump, thump* of the base, not the chaos of sound. People move out of our way as we walk, their eyes flying up to Recon as they step back, letting us pass through the club. It's as if everyone in a three-foot radius can sense the electric power Recon emanates and gives him a wide berth.

When we're just a few feet away, I stop in front of the leather U-shaped sectional right in the middle of the VIP lounge, leaving just the glossy black square coffee table between us. Cora moves up to my side, her shoulder brushing against my arm as we take in the sight before us. Up close, I notice the men are all dressed in similar costumes, but the masks covering their faces are vastly different. Recon sits on the couch next to the male with a fanged skull on his mask, and pats his lap, eyes on Cora.

She's pressed so tightly to me, I feel a shiver move through her. Glancing my way, almost for reassurance, she moves around the low table and settles in Recon's lap, biting her lip as her eyes fall on the man next to her. Fanged Skull Mask reaches out with a gloved hand and brushes her red hair from her shoulder.

Okay. So that's how this is going to go with these guys.

Looking back at the man in the center, I take in his costume. He's wearing the same fatigues and boots as Recon, Fang, and the man next to him, but instead of his sleeves pulled down to his wrists, they're pushed up to reveal thick forearms covered in dark ink. The bits I can make out are exquisitely done. A few floral designs as well as skulls weave around his arm, disappearing into his gloves. Several solid black lines wrap around his tanned arm near his elbow, making me wonder what they mean.

My eyes rake over his body, taking in his thighs and muscled chest, and stop at his eyes. Just like the other men, his eyes are uncovered, but it's pure darkness. Black eyes stare back at me from the unnerving skull face. Recon's mask is a plain ghostly skull, Fang has long sharp canines, and the quiet man next to Reaper looks like his skull's face is slashed through with a cut, forming a long scar over his eye. Reaper's mask is more menacing. The skull looks like it's stitched around the edges of his face and the lower jaw looks like it melts down his neck.

"I hear you requested my company," I say to him, keeping my eyes locked on his, resisting the urge to squirm under his gaze. He's intense. His entire demeanor demands attention. Obedience.

Recon lets out a laugh, but I keep my focus on Reaper.

It's only because I'm watching him that I catch the slight movement under Reaper's mask, like he's smiling.

No. I doubt he's smiling. This guy would smirk, never smile.

Out of the corner of my eye, I see Cora twisting in Recon's lap, angling herself so she can look at Fang by his side.

"Oh, she's cute," the male with the scarred mask next to Reaper says, lifting a hand to me. "I like them feisty."

"Cute little kitty cat," Fang says, and I glance his way. He's large. Not just judging by his long legs, but his build. Broad shoulders and chest. Massive thighs that look like they're testing the seams of his black cargo pants. He points to my mask. "Are you a naughty kitty or a nice one?"

"I'm the kind that draws blood," I purr, my voice smooth as ice.

Scar barks out a laugh, and I watch as the muscles under Fang's tight black shirt ripple with laughter.

"Take that kitty cat mask off and let me see that pretty face," Fang says, his attention lingering on Cora as he runs the back of his gloved fingers over her cheek. His light eyes drops to her full lips, and he lightly touches her bottom lip. "I want to see if you're as lovely as this gorgeous Vixen."

Biting her lip, she seems to melt further into Recon's lap, a smile tugging at the corner of her mouth, making her green eyes glitter.

I turn my attention back to Reaper before me. My belly flutters. The way the lights flash over him creates a menacing glint in his eyes. He lets his gaze drag lazily down my body, boldly taking in my cleavage, greedily drinking in every dip and swell, then stopping between my legs before dropping to my knee boots. With something that resembles hunger, his eyes move back up to my face, the possessive gleam he's not bothering to hide creating a slickness between my thighs.

My cheeks warm, my chest turning red, and I place a hand to the skin. Somehow, his focus seems to narrow in on me even more, like he can sense I find his devouring gaze, his predatory presence, arousing. I lift my arm and his black eyes dart to my hand, watching with laser focus as I remove my mask. Never breaking eye contact, I toss it to the black table between us. My heart pounds as I take in a shallow breath, waiting for one of them to recognize me—for him to—but the only movement from Reaper is the slight tick of muscles under his shirt.

"Beautiful," Scar says, leaning forward to rest his forearms on his thighs, letting his dark eyes move down my body.

Lifting a gloved hand, Reaper turns his palm up, holding it out for me as he leans forward just enough that I can reach him. On instinct, I place my hand in his and his large fingers enclose over my mine. Irritation rolls through me, but I refuse to let him know that I'm pissed at myself for immediately placing my hand in his. For so readily obeying.

Instead of yanking it back in defiance, I make my way around the table until I'm standing directly in front of him. His thumb skims the inside of my wrist, setting off fireworks, the sparkling heat settling low in my core. Still holding my hand, he pats his large thigh with his free hand.

Sit.

CHAPTER 3

DELILAH

REAPER RELEASES MY HAND, and it falls to my side. My skin pricks under his piercing black gaze, his stare cutting through all my layers like knives, making me feel exposed. Like he's seeing under my flesh, to the marrow in my bones and the rich ruby blood in my veins. All the way to my frantically beating heart, fluttering wildly like a trapped bird in my rib cage.

And I'm not sure he likes what he sees.

I let my eyes flicker down to his lap as if I'm assessing the situation, masking my nerves with arrogance and acting a hell of a lot more confident than I feel right now. It's something I'm not used to feeling. Off-center and out of my element. My name, my position in life, demands people obey me. Not the other way around. When I look back up at his face, I swear the skull smirks at me.

"Cat got your tongue?" I ask, my pulse quickening as his eyes narrow, letting me see tanned flesh and black brows. That fluttering in my heart drops, crashing to my belly, the broken pieces of my unease settling as I watch him assess me with those incredible eyes. The lashes framing the almond shape are so black and so thick, it looks like he's wearing makeup.

He shifts a little and I swear he grows even larger as he sits up to his full height, widening his legs just a tad, eating up the space and turning the tension between us up several notches.

Okay. So he is a guy who gets what he wants. Always.

I'm used to men like him. I was raised by one.

Capturing my bottom lip with my teeth, I cock my head to the side, liking how his focus shifts to the pink flesh.

Fine. We can play his game. I'll let him think he has all the power here if his ego needs it. He can have my plump ass in his lap, and I'll allow him this win, just until I figure out what he wants. He may regret it, though.

Turning so that my ass is in his face, I sink down into his lap, my back to his chest. The second I'm settled, Reaper's large arm wraps around my middle, and he pulls me to him, flattening his palm to my belly, pressing my rear against the buckle of his belt. I shift to get situated, wiggling my ass seductively as I settled down.

Before I can even think about the fact I'm sitting in a strange man's lap in the middle of my father's club, his hands move, gripping my thighs, spreading my legs. With my legs hooked over his knees, he widens his own so I'm spread slightly open, my back pressed to his chest. Hot air blasts against my right ear, his head dipping to my neck. My scalp tingles as my hair shifts, his nose pressing to the flesh.

Wait. *Is he smelling me?*

A shiver runs up my spine, my body shuddering. With how close we are, I know he can feel the way my body reacts to him. To his hands placed on the top of my thighs, to the heat seeping through his shirt into my bare back. All my female parts reacting to his very male presence and the trace of woodsy cologne that seems to fill my lungs entirely.

Sucking in a breath, I regret it immediately when my lungs fill with his scent, the intensity of being so surrounded by him, so possessed by him, making me feel heady. My heart stutters as his hands start moving up and down the tops of my thighs, like he's soothing me. After a few frantic heartbeats, my shoulders relax, my spine loosens, and I melt into him until I'm soft against the hard planes of his body.

"Reaper's had his eye on you," Scar says from next to me, and I look over in his direction to see him offering a drink.

Panic needles down my arms, and I glance at Cora to find she's holding a similar drink, chatting with Recon and Fang.

Damn it, Cora. So much for not accepting drinks from strange men.

Turning my focus back on Scar, I say, "You speak for the man beneath me?"

Scar throws his head back, letting out a loud laugh, then pins me with dark eyes. Not as dark as Reaper's, but dark enough. "No one speaks for Reaper," he says. "And you may be in his lap, but that's only because he put you there, Princess."

His words sound like a warning, but it's not lined with a threat. More like a reminder that I have little power here right now. Funny. Because I could get up and leave if I wanted.

But I don't want to.

I twist my head, looking over my shoulder, but I can't see anything other than a menacing gaze.

"Not much of a talker, are you?" I ask, a light tremble running through my body at the way his palms drag over my stockings.

"Here," Scar says, snagging my attention again, offering the drink. "It's just rum and soda."

I give him a flat look. "No secret ingredients?" I ask, even as I take the drink.

Scar laughs again and my lips curve with a grin. His costume may look intimidating, along with the sheer bulk of the guy, but he seems pretty outgoing. "It's not tainted, Princess. We like our girls awake and willing."

Awareness jolts through me, his words making me freeze as I place my lips around the straw. My gaze flickers over to Cora and I nearly choke when I see she's pressed back into Recon's chest, head tilted back, and Fang's gloved hand moves between her legs over the material of her costume.

Well, shit.

So much for our girl code tonight.

"Cora," I hiss, leaning forward, but Scar's powerful arm lashes out, pinning me in place. I grip his forearm looking around to see if anyone notices that my friend's getting some heavy petting in the middle of the club's VIP lounge.

Scar's eyes darken. "Cora seems quite willing." He gestures to my friend who now has Recon's hand cupping her breast as Fang cups between her legs. His deep voice trembles through me. "Are you?"

"Willing?" I ask, tearing my eyes off my friend to meet Scar's gaze. "Or pliant?"

"*Com*pliant," Scar says.

My tongue feels thick in my mouth, and I swallow. "Complaint?"

"Submissive." The word rolls over me like a caress. "Eagerly spreading your legs for us. Opening your mouth for us."

My stomach drops. The thundering of my heart beats between my legs, a wild feeling tearing its way through me as I take in his words.

"Wow," I say, trying to breathe normally. Glancing over my shoulder at Reaper, I meet his smoldering black eyes. "No dropping subtle hints with this guy, huh?"

"We don't have time for subtleties," Scar says. His arm slides from around my middle, snapping my attention back to him. He drags a gloved finger down my bare arm, leaving a trail of fire down my skin. "And we don't like waiting around for indecisive people."

In other words, decide or we move on.

"How about it, Princess?" Scar's gaze travels to Cora. "Do you want us to make you feel good?"

Excitement surges to my clit, leaving me throbbing at the thought. At his word choice.

Us. These guys want us. *Both* of us.

All *four* of these guys.

Taking a long pull of my drink, I let his offer slip seductively through me. I lean forward to set my drink down, but Reaper's hands tightens, keeping me in place. A weird, feverish shiver starts low in my belly and slips up my spine. I settle back, relaxing, allowing him to keep me pinned to his chest.

My gaze falls to Cora, and I wonder what that would be like? To be so free. To not have to be so controlled all the time. Abandon my duty—my fucking title—as Rune Gavin's daughter for a night and give myself permission to enjoy life. Be overtaken by someone powerful, larger than me. To not be so protected by my father's name. The thought of letting go of my obligations for a night splinters me with longing.

"What do you say, Princess?" Scar asks, his eyes gliding over my body as intimately as if it were his hands. "Do you want to play with us?"

Reaper must feel me tense, because his calming movements stop. His gloved palm slides up to my inner thigh, and grazes, just barely over my pussy before he slides it up my belly, between my breasts. His touch sends fire up my spine, intensifying as it travels up my body. Stopping just at the base of my throat, his fingers press into my flesh and he pulls me into him even more until my back is molded to his hard chest, the outline of his pecs under my shoulders a reminder of how powerful and masculine he is underneath me.

My pulse quickens, the thrumming echoing in my head. I know he can feel my heart beating wildly at the thought of them. *All* of them.

Hot breaths fan over my neck as Reaper leans down to my ear. With a deep masculine voice that sends a shiver through me, he whispers against the sensitive flesh, "Come play with us, Kitten. I want to hear you purr."

CHAPTER 4

Delilah

"*I* WANT TO HEAR *you purr.*"

That voice.

Something niggles the back of my brain, the gruff voice reminding me of someone, *something*, but I can't place it.

My lungs heave with the effort to take in air. Instinctively, I try to press my legs together, but Reaper's thick thighs keep my legs parted. An ache blooms between my legs and it's like he can sense it because his other hand slides up my thigh and a thick gloved finger skims over my pussy, rubbing me lightly over the material. A light moan slips past my lips.

"Do you like to play, Kitten?" Reaper asks against my ear.

"I don't think she's ever played with so many," Scar says, like he can hear what Reaper's whispering.

"Four's a lot," I manage, gripping his wrist to make him stop touching me, but instead of removing his hand, he just pauses the light stroking, keeping his finger pressed to me. I grit my teeth, fighting the urge to spread my legs wider and rock into his touch. "You're right, I've never been with that many at once."

I've never had sex with more than one man, *ever*, but I keep that tidbit to myself. My over protective father made sure my love life was next to nothing and having sex was impossible. No one wanted to come within ten feet of me, much less lay their hands on me out of fear of losing it. Until Dave, that is. But he was Rune approved. And to my disappointment, Dave was rather lame in bed. At least with me. Imagine my surprise when I found his secretary in our massive bed, dressed in *my* fucking silk nightie with her hands tied to *my* bedpost.

God, what would he think if he found out I was with four men?

A dark pleasure crackles through me, liking the thought of my ex-husband knowing I was fucked by so many men in one night. It would serve him right for telling me I didn't please him in bed. That I wasn't adventurous. That I wasn't *enough*.

I swear Scar smiles with the way his mask shifts around his mouth and wrinkles crease around his eyes like he can sense what I'm thinking. This stranger in a mask is more in tune with me than my fucking ex-husband was.

"Always a first," Scar says, glancing at where Reaper has his finger resting. Locking his focus on my lips, he reaches out and runs the back of his gloved fingers over my outer thigh, like he's testing my reaction. My nipples tighten and my back arches as Reaper strokes his finger over me again. "I promise I'll be gentle, Princess."

"I won't," Reaper growls in my ear.

Reaper shifts, pressing me further into him. Underneath me, I feel his thick erection along my backside. Between my legs grows slick with want, making me tilt my hips, but it just digs his length harder into me.

God, how I want to give in to the temptation. Surrender myself to them. To this gnawing desire snaking through my belly.

With a trembling hand, I grip the glass, bringing the straw to my lips, and take a long pull of the drink, but the burning liquor does nothing to tame the fire building in my belly. When it's empty, Scar removes it from my grasp and sets it on the table in front of us.

Reaper's soft nudge to my ear sends a wave of longing through me. "But I promise you'll enjoy how rough I'll fuck you."

Scar laughs again, his hand slipping over my thigh to grip right next to where Reaper's finger is pressed. The sensation sends another jolt of desire crashing through me. His touch only intensifies the longing building within, making it hard to want anything other than Reaper to press harder. For Scar's hand to join his. For them to do more.

Shit. I *like* this. Both of their large hands on my thigh. What would it feel like to have their large, strong hands in different places? I imagine Recon resting his hand next to Scar's on my leg. Fang slipping his up higher. Higher still.

Fear trickles down my arms, and I shut the thought down. What am I doing? If my father found out these men were attempting to get Cora and me to go with them, he'd kill them. Four men taking advantage of his daughter and his little Cora?

And that's how he'd see it. Instead of us going willingly, taking part in a night of pure lust of our own free will, he'd think they coerced us, or worse, forced us to go with them. He'd fucking destroy them if he thought that.

The only reason Dave is still alive after he broke my heart is because he's my father's lawyer. Dave's too important to dispose of and too many questions would arise if he was found dead in an ally. Not that he isn't replaceable, but in my father's profession, loyalty is hard to find. Even if Dave wasn't loyal to me, he proved he's reliable and trustworthy to my father. These guys? They could be anyone.

The thought rushes a tidal wave of unease over me, dampening my curiosity. These men could be my father's enemies.

Calm down, Delilah. Not every single person is a threat.

My father's words crash through my head. *Keep your eyes open and your heart closed.*

I don't need my heart for this, I think as I meet Scar's dark eyes. Just an open mind and open legs.

Biting my lip, I suck in a shaky breath, trying to center my thoughts. Scar's observing me, waiting for a response. I watch as his gaze moves to my breasts before asking, "Who are you?"

"Does it matter?" Scar asks, still eyeing my body. I wonder if he's thinking about what Reaper said a moment ago. Fucking me roughly.

"It does if you plan on coming on me," I retort, feeling sparks tingle up my back as Reaper's hand digs into the soft place between my thighs. My teeth sink into my bottom lip harder, excitement dampening the fabric under his finger as he teases.

"On you?" Reaper asks, laughing darkly. "Kitten, I'm going to be coming *in* you."

Scar inches in even closer, his thigh hitting my backside. "And I'm going to take your mouth hard. Make you choke on my cock until my cum is spilling from between your lips."

My breath rushes out, the image taking over all rational thoughts. I lick my lips and if I could see Scar's mouth under his mask, I know I'd catch him smiling at my reaction.

"Who are you?" I ask again, blinking the images away.

Get a grip, Delilah. I'm Rune Gavin's daughter, for god's sake. A powerful man who's trained me from an early age to trust my instincts, take control of every situation and turn it to my benefit. Even if the odds are stacked against me.

I've spent my entire life building up my father's empire. Protecting it by doing every single thing he tells me, when he tells me, and I do it with a smile on my face. I'm the only person on this entire planet my father trusts completely. The one person he needs.

As asked, I went to school to manage his finances because he needed me to. He sent Cora as well because she has to abide by his demands as much as I do. Between Cora and me; we know his finances better than he does. We're the backbone of his corporation hiding what he truly does under mountains of numbers. Under paperwork and mergers. Under the layers and layers of bodies we stepped over to build my father's company to be the highest grossing network of hotels and clubs this side of the country. Hell, in the entire Western Hemisphere, by the time I'm done with it.

These men are nothing to me. Nothing to my goals of becoming even more powerful than my father. As shitty as my brief marriage to Dave was, that year taught me many things. The first being everything my father instilled in me was true. Only I am responsible for and can take care of my needs. I can't trust anyone. Not him. Not Cora, whom I've known most of my life.

Not even myself sometimes, it seems.

Because I'm quickly losing to these four men who say they want me.

Reaper's finger feathers over me again, making me bite back a moan.

"We're not here to hurt you, Princess," Scar says, leaning into the couch, throwing his arm over the back.

My eyes track his movement, drawn to the thick bands of muscles beneath his shirt. These guys are all muscles and hard planes, making me wonder if they're bodyguards or just obsessed with the gym. Something tells me they're more than that.

They're darker.

Cora's giggle pulls my attention from Scar. Our eyes meet and she raises her brows in question, silently asking if I'm okay. I give her a slight nod, quirking a brow at the hand still between her legs, making her smirk.

Not like I have room to judge considering.

"Just here to play?" I ask.

Scar tilts his head to the side. "Something like that."

"Do you guys make it a habit of prowling around clubs, searching for women to fill with your come?" I clutch Reaper's wrist tighter, that desperate need threatening to consume, but he ignores my grip and continues to feather my pussy with light touches, sending electric bolts of pleasure through me.

"Kitten, we're always on the hunt," Reaper says, making me turn my head to look over my shoulder. His dark eyes gleam toxic, reflecting the streams of pink neon light from overhead. "And you're our prey."

CHAPTER 5

DELILAH

REAPER MOVES THE HAND at my throat up to my jaw and clasps tightly, pressing his face to my ear. "Are you ready for us?"

Next to us, Cora squirms in Recon's lap, moving her hips to meet the hand between her thighs. My eyes grow wide and I glance around again. Either no one cares enough to look at what's happening or no one dares. I have a feeling no one dares question these men, which sends excitement surging through my veins. Watching Cora squirm in Recon's lap as Fang moves his hand over her, builds up a tight coiling sensation in my core.

"Not out here," I say, watching Cora. *Jesus, girl.* I know she's not drunk. At least not on alcohol because we've barely had any drinks. Worry eats at my middle, wondering if they did drug the beverages. But I seem okay, even if my skin is buzzing, but it's only from nerves, not drugs. As if she can sense my fear, Cora lifts her head and catches my eye again. She looks sober enough, just a little dazed, no doubt from the pressure of Fang's hand between her legs.

"Are we doing this?" she asks, her voice a sharp plea.

I realize if I asked, she'd walk away with me. But can I really walk away? My brain screams that I don't know these men, I haven't even seen their faces, but between my legs throbs at the thrill of the unknown.

I don't know them. They could be dangerous. Fuck, they probably *are* dangerous and I think that's part of the excitement. I've never done this. Hell, I've never done anything so reckless.

But oh how I want to.

"Yeah," I say, straightening my back. Reaper's hands fall away as I push myself up off his lap. Spinning to face him, I catch his black eyes and see the corners crinkling, no doubt with a satisfied smirk. "I want to play."

The four men stand at once, Recon, placing Cora gently down in front of him. When Reaper stands, he towers over me, at least a few inches taller than Recon, and even more than Scar and Fang.

"Names," I say, looking each man in the eye. "And the masks come off."

"Masks stay on," Reaper says with such finality, my breath rushes out. I swear it's like he pulls the air from my lungs every time he speaks.

"But you can have my name," Fang says. "I want to hear you scream it when you come."

Cora breathes out a *Jesus H Christ* at my side and grips my hand.

"Name's Viper," Fang says, and I almost laugh.

"Viper," I repeat and look at Recon.

He brushes a curl away from Cora's cheek and grips her chin, speaking his name directly to her. "Breaker."

A rush of air leaves her as he runs his large thumb over her bottom lip.

I look over at Scar. "And what name will I be screaming when you make me come?"

"Fuck," he breathes, adjusting himself. "I like this one, Reaper." He steps in close and leans down between Cora and me. "The name is Striker."

Cora grins. "Fun names, boys." She glances around the club and it's like all the chaotic noise bleeds back in. It's suddenly too loud. We'd been in such a bubble that the music and nearby laughter seized to exist. "So, where are we doing this?"

Reaper grips my hand in his large one and pulls me forward. With me still holding onto Cora, she follows with the newly named Breaker, Viper, and Striker at our heels. We weave through the club and again, people part to allow us to pass, eyes moving from the men to Cora and me between them. My skin pricks, not liking the many looks we're getting, but I ignore their curious stares and hold my head up high as we walk to the back of the club. When we reach a large metal door, we all stop. Next to the heavy door stands one of the clubs bouncer's.

God, please don't recognize us.

The bouncer's eyes dart to me, but he looks back at Reaper, who leans in and says something. The massive man opens the door and steps aside, allowing us entry.

Over my shoulder, I glance at Cora to see her raised brows. We both have the same thought.

Who do these men know, that the doorman is just letting them into the private lounge?

Please don't let it be my father.

The door shuts behind us and the loud thumping music instantly dims, reduced to just a faint pulse, leaving a hollowed-out ringing in my ears. Cora places her hands on my shoulders and peers around me as Viper, Striker, and Breaker walk further into the room.

The space is large. In the center are more couches made of white leather with dark glossy tables nearby. Just like the rest of the club, its dark except for the blue glow coming from decorative lights on the walls and overhead. Recon... No, Breaker, walks to a table and grabs two glasses and a bottle of champagne.

"Drinks?" he asks and pops the top, making me jolt so hard that I crash into Reaper at my side.

He reaches down and runs his thumb along my jawline, making my breath swoosh out of me. "Don't be nervous, little Kitty," he says, turning his voice smooth and velvety. "We certainly don't want to hurt you."

"God, yes," Cora says, stepping forward to take the flute from Viper and emptying it in one gulp. She holds it out for more.

"One more," Reaper says, nodding to Breaker as Striker and Viper move to sit on the U-shaped sectional at the center of the room.

Once the men are settled, Viper pats his lap. "Come here sweet Vixen," he says to Cora, reaching out to grasp her by the waist and pulling her down. "Let's continue what we started."

She giggles and falls to his lap, reaching up and behind her to grip his neck as her head falls back to his shoulder. Viper grips her thighs and spreads her legs wide, using his own to hold her open, much like Reaper had been doing with me. Breaker sits down next to him, inching in close so he can easily run his hand down her torso. Her mouth opens and her gaze flickers to me as his hand lowers and skims between her legs.

Jesus H Christ is right.

"You're a skittish little kitty," Striker says, pulling me forward.

We stop in front of the couches next to Cora and the two men. Reaper slips between us and settles down on the center couch, pulling me so I'm across his lap, his hand landing on the top of my thigh and sliding down between my legs, but not touching me there. Striker moves in behind me, sitting next to Reaper on the other side, making the couch dip with his weight, and me slip into the space between the two men's thighs.

"You're going to watch for now," Reaper says.

My eyes dart to Reaper's. The black seems to glimmer with mischief, making my stomach dip. Heat presses into my shoulder and I gasp, so shocked at the sensation of warm skin against mine, that I turn. Striker has pulled his mask up so just his mouth and chin are exposed, revealing warm skin and wide, full lips. His eyes meet mine and in the brighter room I see they're a rich brown, cast with an almost purple hue in the blue lights. He smirks, making my eyes fall back to his mouth pressed to my bare shoulder.

His lips pull into an even larger grin. "Reaper wants you to watch, Princess." His eyes move back to Cora and I turn too.

Recon...no Breaker, has pulled his mask up too, showing off full lips and a smooth dark-skinned jawline that's so perfectly cut, I know he must be devastating under that mask.

Cora's hand lightly touches his jaw as he encloses his mouth over hers, licking the seam. She parts her lips and his tongue slips inside.

My thighs press together, tightness building in my core at the sight of his tongue moving in and out of her mouth like he's gently fucking her. The prickling heat of Reaper's focus tells me he's watching my reaction, but I can't seem to look away, even as Scar's... no, Striker's hand slips around my belly, moving up to cup my breast. My nipple tightens under my bra as he gently kneads, making me arch into his touch.

"Keep watching, Princess," Striker whispers into my skin. "I want you so wet, you're dripping for us."

His words send another surge through me and I focus on Cora as instructed. Breaker's hands are roaming everywhere, between her thighs, up to her breasts where Viper has his hands as well. The two men's gloved hands brush each other as they move over Cora, and I wonder for the first time if they will touch each other. Desire flares through me at the thought.

"What are you thinking, Kitten?" Reaper asks, shifting beneath me. His hard length jerks under my thigh and I squirm as even more excitement sears through me, liking way too much that he's aroused for me. Because of me.

Because of us. Cora and I. Because of this entire situation.

Striker pinches my hard nipple through the material, his other hand slipping up to do the same to my other breast. I realize now my hands have moved of their own accord, and one is gripping Reaper's thigh, the other pressing into his hard abdomen.

"Tell us what you're thinking," Reaper says, more demanding this time.

"Be gentle with her, Reap," Striker says behind me, almost like a plea. One hand leaves my breast, and he pulls my hair back to place a kiss on the back of my neck.

"Do you guys touch each other too?" I ask, my head dropping to give him access, still watching Cora and the way Breaker's and Viper's hands seem to work together, gradually removing her heels, then slipping her leotard and green leggings off until she's completely naked, her pale skin and freckles on full display.

"Shit. She's gorgeous," Striker murmurs behind me.

Viper pauses long enough to remove his gloves and tosses them aside, revealing pale skin and large, calloused hands. Breaker, sensing Viper's intentions, follows suit, removing his own gloves. As Viper pulls Cora back onto his lap, Breaker grips her thighs, shoving them open to reveal her bare pussy, right before Viper drives a finger inside her, his hand gently cradling her mound.

With a gasp, Cora meets my eyes.

Fuck it, right?

Right. I'm about to watch my friend get fucked.

Thoroughly.

My heart hammers against my rib cage.

"Do you have a problem with that?" Striker says and for a second, I forgot I had asked a question.

Ripping my eyes from Cora getting finger fucked by Viper and kissed by Breaker, I look at Reaper. "You guys fuck each other?"

I swear he cocks a brow under his mask. "Is that a problem?" His body grows hard underneath me as he tenses. "If it's a fucking problem, you can leave now."

My stomach dips at his immediate defensive tone. *No.* Not a problem. I've never been in the room with *other* people fucking, in general.

Licking my lips, I say, "I'm just curious if we're the only ones who will have cum pouring from us."

Striker's harsh laugh sends a heated breath fanning the back of my neck and my pussy pulses.

Biting my lip, I steal a glance back at Breaker and Viper. Breaker releases Cora's thighs, but Viper's hand remains between her legs as Breaker stands and begins unbuttoning his pants. Still fingering Cora, Viper leans forward, pushing her upright just as Breaker releases his long, thick cock. He's fucking perfect. *Huge.* Before Cora can part her lips and accept him into her mouth, Viper leans forward, pulls up the stretchy fabric of his mask, uncovering the auburn stubble along his jawline, and sucks Breaker's cock into his mouth.

All I hear is Cora's gasp just as, "Holy shit," slips past my lips.

CHAPTER 6

DELILAH

He's beautiful. The way he's delicately holding Breaker, receiving him into his mouth, cheeks hollowing out as he sucks him in deep. Breaker cradles his head, helping him bob up and down on his cock, hips gently rocking forward.

They aren't new to this. They aren't experimenting tonight or just having fun. The way Viper touches Breaker means this is a regular occurrence between them. Reaper's defensive response makes sense now. This is something he's protecting.

These men *mean* something to him.

Striker kisses the back of my neck as I eat up the sight of Viper and the thick cock slipping wetly between his lips. A desperate growl escapes Breaker and his hips jut forward, his large hand holding Viper's head in place, making Viper's eyes flutter and water as he chokes.

Warmth rushes between my thighs, want building up even tighter as Breaker weaves his fingers into Cora's hair when she leans in and kisses his hip. With a *pop*, his cock slips out of Viper's mouth and Cora leans forward to suck on the head of his dick. He's so big, she can't fit him all the way in her mouth, so she licks along his length, circling around the head as Viper grips him at the root and strokes.

A deep guttural sound rumbles from behind me, making me turn my head to find Striker watching the scene before us. His hand still possessively cups my breasts, kneading as he skims warm lips over my shoulder and neck with light kisses, sparks of want flying through my body as he works his way up my neck.

None of them are new to this. There's an intense connection sizzling through the air. These men aren't just friends. They're connected in some way. Like Cora and I.

I squirm in Reaper's lap, fire igniting within me. The realization we've added to something that's already existed, our presence not taking away from the fire that these men share, creates a dark, provocative want within me. I want to be a part of this. Want to feel the same electric surge between them catch fire to my skin and consume me.

Reaper releases his grip on my thigh as I continue to squirm, between my legs throbbing so intensely, it's become an ache, and cups my jaw tightly, ripping a surprised gasp from my throat.

"Striker," he says roughly. "Kiss her. Now."

On command, Striker covers Reaper's hand with his and yanks me into him, angling my head back toward him. His lips crash against mine. The position makes my lips part. He takes advantage and slips his tongue in, tasting me. A breathy groan escapes him and his warm, minty breath floods my senses, mixing with the dark warm scent of Reaper. The searing kiss makes my head swirl, all thoughts draining away until I'm rocking, tilting my hips, reaching behind me to grip the back of his head, dragging his mouth closer. I feel hands move around me—Striker—and he reaches between my legs. Instinctively, I part them and let him slip a hand under my body suit, the need to be touched making me pant into his mouth. He presses to my folds over the pantyhose and curses.

"She's got on those stockings," Striker growls, breaking our kiss. "I can't stroke her pussy with them on."

"Up," Reaper orders, and I slip off his lap as Striker lifts me to stand. Pushing off the couch, Reaper grips my jaw again and runs his gloved thumb over my lips. "I'm going to watch this pretty mouth get fucked tonight."

My breath rushes out just as Striker reaches between my legs and unbuttons the bodysuit, the snap of the buttons coming undone making me jolt.

"These boots are sexy as hell," Striker says, sliding a hand down my thigh, "but we need to remove them to get these stockings off."

"No, they stay on," Reaper says. Reaching to his side, he pulls something from his belt and my eyes grow wide, my heart stuttering in my chest when I see him pop open a knife. "Cut them off."

I open my mouth to scream, but his hand clamps down hard over my lips, muffling the sound. Locking me in place with his dark gaze, he leans in close and says, "We'd never dream of hurting you, Kitten."

"The pantyhose, though. They're getting destroyed," Striker says with a chuckle, plucking the knife from Reaper's hand. A second later, I feel a tug and then the restricting fabric between my legs suddenly releases.

Reaper lets me go and backs away. I look down to see Striker has cut the seam of my pantyhose to give them access, leaving me completely exposed. I press my thighs together, feeling just how wet I am as my pulse flutters. Reaper's piercing gaze between my legs sends desire flaring through me.

"Beautiful," Reaper rasps, sitting back down and gesturing for me to sit back on his lap.

"Let's get this off you, Princess," Striker says, running his hands down my back and gripping the material of my bodysuit.

Before I can protest, it's lifted and pulled over my head, then falling to the floor at my feet, leaving me in just my black bra, the cut pantyhose, and leather knee boots. I'd feel ridiculous if it weren't for the way Reaper's eyes move over me, drinking in every inch of skin. My belly, the curve of my hips, my full breasts.

"Fuck me," Striker grates out, moving to stand in front of me. He grips my chin, angling my head back to meet his warm eyes. A devious grin curls his lip. "You look good enough to eat."

A strangled cry drags my attention to Cora. Breaker's on his knees, his head between her legs, hands splayed on her open thighs as Viper grips her hair and thrusts roughly into her mouth, her eyes tearing. One of her small hands rests on his hip, the other's holding onto Breaker, fingers curled into the black fabric of his head covering.

She's loving this. I know she's been with many men, she doesn't leave out any details when she tells me about her weekend dates, but to see her taking him so well, so submissively, shoots desire through my core.

Like he can sense my fiery gaze, Viper casts a look my way, our eyes locking as he thrusts into her mouth. His lips curve with a wolfish grin. "You get this cock next, Sweetheart."

Striker groans, watching me watch Cora. "You want that, Princess? A cock in your mouth while your pussy gets devoured?"

"As I fuck her from behind," Reaper says.

"Fuck," Viper groans, head thrown back now, driving into Cora's mouth harder, making her choke on her moan. "You're too good at this, you naughty little Vixen."

I glance back at Reaper. *As I fuck her from behind.* The image floods my mind and I can't let it go. Reaper thrusting into me, my legs spread with Striker's mouth on my pussy, and Viper's cock down my throat.

"You want that," Reaper says like he can see what I'm imagining. "Us."

I nod.

He pulls me down to his lap again and Striker falls to his knees in front of us, ripping off his gloves and capturing my mouth with a frenzied hunger.

Suddenly, hands are everywhere. Reaper's coarse fabric-covered hands pulling my legs open, hooking them back over his thick thighs. Striker's warm fingers between my legs, slipping through my wet folds with wicked intent. Rough gloved fingers wrapping tightly around my throat as I part my lips, allowing Striker to delve his tongue deep into my mouth, ravishing me with a passionate kiss. I open myself wider for him and let him slip those warm fingers inside me.

"Shit," he curses. "She's fucking drenched, Reap."

"*Hmm,*" Reaper grunts out behind me, gripping my throat tighter. "Tell me what she tastes like."

Striker slips lower, and I grip Reaper's forearms, readying myself. When Striker's searing lips skim my sensitive flesh, I cry out, bowing my back as his tongue slides over my clit.

"Like honey," Striker says, then his tongue slides along my aching skin, making me tremble with pleasure. Reaper's grip at my throat tightens, constricting my breath, making me arch against him. I grip his forearms, digging my fingers hard into his bare skin, my nails clawing at his flesh as delicious heat rolls through me in waves.

"My little Kitten has claws," Reaper growls against my ear. "But she doesn't know I like the pain."

Striker slips his tongue deep into my opening and I groan as he plunges it in and out like he's fucking me. Consumed with a flood of desire, I try to open my legs even wider, longing curling up in my belly so tight, I know I won't last much longer. He grips my thighs, pushing them up until I fall back into Reaper's chest, giving Striker full access. He takes advantage and swipes his tongue from my ass up to my clit, groaning as he does.

"Reap, you got to taste this pussy," Striker says, driving two fingers back into me. Slick wet sounds fill the air, mixing with Cora's soft moans, and Viper's panting grunts.

It's too much to take in. Reaper's hand at my throat, Striker's fingers moving in and out, his tongue at my clit, circling, exploring what I like, then sucking me into his hot mouth. The dirty words pouring from him when he releases me with a slick *pop*. Cora's choked cries beside me as Breaker devours her and Viper fucks her mouth. It's all too overwhelming and I writhe under Striker's tight grasp, barely aware that I'm tilting my hips to meet his mouth that's pulling, *demanding,* my pleasure, when suddenly the world breaks away and I cry out.

Reaper's grip tightens even more as my orgasm rips through my body, the pressure, the complete lack of my control in this moment, adding to the already intense pleasure Striker's ripping from me. I try to close my trembling legs around Striker's head, curling into myself as the waves consume me, but they both have such a tight a hold of me, keeping me splayed open.

"I can't," I whisper when I realize Striker is determined to tear another orgasm from me. "I can't."

Cora's muffled cry followed by Breaker's dark laugh sends a fire to my clit, but Striker takes mercy and pulls away, sitting upright. His satisfied gaze travels up my flushed body to my eyes. My release coats his mouth and he smirks, then lets out a rough groan as he grips himself through his pants.

A feral, uncaged feeling surges through me, causing a tremble to move down my back, desperate for the taste of him. I want him in my mouth, thrusting past my lips, soaking me with his rough desire. All of them. I want, *need*, them all everywhere. The craving is so dark, so animalistic, it's like all my senses are overtaken by this wild need. By *them*.

Cora sits upright, gasping when Viper pulls his dick from her mouth. He bends down, gripping her hips and flipping her over so she's on her hands and knees, facing me. Our eyes lock. Breaker kneels behind her, caressing her naked body, smoothing his long fingers over her pale flesh, pressing his thumbs into the indents on her lower back, like he's cherishing her. Viper places a knee next to them on the couch, bending over to kiss her round ass before he tilts his head to the side and sucks Breaker back into his mouth briefly, then releasing his large dick with an obscene *pop*.

Cora's gaze drifts to Reaper, locking on him as she crawls forward. The second I see her intent, a tendril of inky blackness slithers through me. Before she can reach Reaper, I tilt sideways and catch her lips with mine.

"That's it, Tiny Thing," Breaker breathes. "Kiss her lush mouth."

"You taste my cock on her lips, Sweetheart?" Viper rasps.

With a startled cry, Cora breaks our kiss and gives me wide, shocked eyes.

I resist rolling my own. Out of everything that's happening, me kissing her is a shock? She leans forward and places another light kiss on my lips, testing it out. She backs away and her eyes move from my mouth to my eyes when she sees it.

Reaper is mine and mine alone.

CHAPTER 7

DELILAH

CORA AND I HAVE never kissed. Fuck, I've never kissed another woman before.

But my blood sizzles, the need to have her lips back on mine as shocking as it is desperate.

With a knowing smirk, Cora leans forward and captures my mouth again, urging my lips apart with her hot tongue. I open, letting her explore. The kiss is gentle, but grows demanding the longer it lasts. Each sweep into my mouth is more heated than the last and I sink into the sensation. Into her sweet taste mixing with the faint, masculine flavor of Viper still on her tongue.

"Spread wider," Breaker growls.

I break our kiss long enough to see him positioning himself at her entrance. She arches her back, tilting her ass upward, giving him easy access before her lips meet mine again, but I keep my eyes open.

I want to see all of this.

"Fuck," Breaker grates, leaning forward to grip her shoulder. His hips move forward slightly and there's a part of me that wishes I could see him easing into her. "Breathe out, Little Red. Let me in."

She releases a soft mewl as Breaker drives into her from behind, using her shoulder to thrust in deeply.

"Fuck," she gasps into my mouth and I eat the word, devouring her soft cries as her body melts to accept him. He pulls out, then thrusts forward again.

"Jesus, he's big." Cora groans against my lips, each one growing louder as he drives faster.

I lift a hand to cup the feminine line of her jaw, marveling at just how different she feels and tastes from the men I've kissed in my life. From Dave. From Striker. She's all soft curves and sweet skin. Her eyes scrunch tightly closed, and I watch as her brows turn down, taking in every sensation she's being given. My kiss and Breaker's rough thrusts.

I break our kiss, want curling up in my middle as Breaker shifts to angle himself deeper. She releases a small sound as he drives in, using her hips to pull her onto him, and I imagine what he must feel like. I saw for myself. He is big. Thick. And he's not being gentle.

"Kiss her again," Reaper demands and I glance at his inky black eyes before obeying.

My tongue delves deep into her mouth, knowing he's watching. Electric cracks in the air as he absorbs the sight of us. I breathe into her mouth, losing myself to the clawing desire snaking through my belly, wanting his approval. Loving the spine-tingling intensity of his sharp focus.

After a moment, I release her mouth and feel warm fingers grip my chin, pulling my face upward. Desire twists through me again. Meeting my eyes, Viper leans over and lowers his mouth to mine. He takes a long slow sweep of my mouth, moving his tongue over mine. He tastes of soda and something else. Something richer. Maybe it's Breaker.

Viper deepens the kiss, weaving his fingers into my hair, snapping my head back. This kiss is demanding, taking, controlling. So different from Cora's. He's rough where she was smooth, his tongue forceful and possessive, contrasting with her gentle desire. Even Striker's passionate kiss didn't feel like such a claiming. Stroking my mouth with his tongue like he was asking me for his pleasure rather than demanding it the way Viper is.

Right when I think I might fall into Viper's dark, sensual need, just as it swirls around me, pushing past my barriers, he eases up and releases me. My head swirls, my heart beating heavily.

"Oh Jesus," Cora whines, dropping her head to the couch cushion. Breaker drives deep into her, his fingers digging into her shoulder, relentlessly seeking his release. Her fingers curl into the leather and I grip her hand, knowing she needs some sort of connection besides the rough fucking Breaker's giving her. Our fingers intertwine and she huffs out another groan as her entire body jolts forward from his rough thrusts.

"She's ready," Reaper says, his cold tone weaving around my lungs and squeezing. Over my shoulder, our eyes lock. "Viper. Take her mouth."

The throbbing between my legs intensifies as understanding pools low in my belly.

Viper cups my jaw, sliding his calloused thumb over my bottom lip, the gentle touch at odds with how rough he was a moment ago.

"Ready, Sweetheart?" he asks, his thumb slipping past my lips as he grasps my hair in his other fist, tilting my head back to meet his eyes. I think they're blue, maybe green. It's hard to tell in the low light. The stubble on his cheeks hints his hair is a dark brown or maybe an auburn. The hard set of his jaw lets me know he's a bit rough. Not just in bed, but in life too. But as he slips his thumb in and out of my mouth, I know he can be gentle if he wants.

Maybe he just doesn't want to.

Not right now.

"Open for me, Sweetheart," Viper says, releasing my hair so he can guide himself to my mouth.

"Open for him, Kitten," Reaper growls. "Let me see how well you take his cock."

I break eye contact, looking down at his length inches from my face, parting my lips, complying with Reaper's instructions. His large hand strokes up and down his shaft, almost lewdly. My heart hammers with anticipation as heat blooms between my legs. He's big, girthy with a slight curve.

Thick fingers whisper through my hair as Reaper curls it into a fist at the back of my head, jerking my head back. With his hand still at my throat, Reaper now has complete control over me as he guides me toward Viper's dick.

"Tongue out," Striker says from his position on the floor next to me, pulling my chin down, his own hand joining with Viper's at my jawline. It's strangely intimate, all these hands on me, guiding me. "That's it, Princess," he says as I open my mouth. "What a good girl you are, opening up for his cock."

Viper grips his dick roughly and hits my tongue with the tip, slapping the head against it as he growls out a strangled sound.

Pre-cum gathers on his slit and he slips the head over my lips, painting me with his essence. That wild clawing returns.

Grows. Reaper's grip tightens in my hair and Striker pulls my jaw, moving me forward.

"Fuck her mouth," Reaper orders, his rough tone combined with his harsh demand burning through my veins. He shifts, positioning himself so he can watch, making his hard length dig into my backside.

Hot fingers slip over my pussy just as Viper slides his dick into my mouth. Salty earthiness floods my tongue and I groan, loving the sensation of Striker's fingers slipping back into me as Viper's cock hits the back of my throat making my eyes tear.

"Fuck," Viper breathes. He withdraws and moves in deep again, barely giving me a moment to breathe.

"Take his cock all the way, Princess," Striker says, his voice growing husky as he watches Viper thrust back into my mouth. His fingers curl up and his thumb brushes my clit. My throaty moan makes Viper's head fall back and a groan slip past his lips.

"Such a good girl for us," Striker says. "Look at how sweetly she opens for you."

Hot breaths fan my ear as Reaper leans down. Scorching heat bursts against my earlobe and I know he's pulled his mask up now too. I want to turn to see the smallest inch of his flesh, but he's holding me still by my throat and hair, allowing Viper to thrust forward into my mouth that Striker's still holding open. I hollow my cheeks, trying to suck him back in, desperate for more whispered praises, needing the worshiping feel of their eyes as I follow their lead.

"Reap, she's fucking pure bliss," Viper groans.

My eyes water as he hits deeply, the head of his cock at the back of my throat making me gag. Saliva gathers in my mouth and I choke, my throat constricting. He holds himself there for a second, the need for air making my pulse quicken, before pulling out all the way. I suck in air, my pussy thrumming with want, even as Striker pushes another finger inside me, using his thumb to slick my wetness up to my clit.

It's not enough. I want *more.*

"Oh fuck," Cora cries from next to me, and I realize I'm still holding her hand. "I'm going to come."

"Come on my cock, sweet little whore," Breaker grates out.

My pussy clenches around Striker's fingers. I turn my head to watch before Viper can drive back in.

"Yes," Cora whimpers, her forehead down on the couch cushion. "Oh, god."

"Shit, she's so tight," Breaker says, pounding into her. "Tight, dirty little whore wants my cum, don't you?"

"Fuck yes," she screams, her back arching as she pulls herself up, bracing herself on her forearms. "Fill me up, baby."

My pussy flutters.

"My nasty little Princess likes to watch her friend get fucked," Striker says, driving his fingers in deep so that I arch my back, sinking my teeth into my lower lip.

"I'm going to fill you up, Little Red," Breaker rasps. A glimmer of sweat gleams on his neck, his jaw popping like he's trying to hold back until she's finished.

"Oh fuck," she breathes, her body shaking, her hand tightening on mine.

Reaper lets out a dark chuckle that scrapes up my spine as Cora cries out again. The hand at my throat, drops and I feel more than see him reach for her. An angry cry builds in my throat, and I turn sideways right before Viper presses his cock to my lips. What had felt like a vise grip before immediately releases me everywhere as the three men's hands fall away when I jerk out of their grasps. Viper backs away the same moment Striker's fingers slip from me. I twist on Reaper's lap, letting go of Cora's hand and grip Reaper's wrist right before he can touch her.

Over my shoulder, his black eyes seem to grow even darker when our gazes collide. My eyes fall to his exposed skin, and a shiver runs through me at the sight of his jawline. His tawny skin is deeply tanned, like he spends hours outside, enhancing his perfectly chiseled jaw. I somehow knew he'd be beautiful, yet I'm still shocked at his soft, pouty lips, turned down into a serious frown. Dark stubble covers his jawline and two deep scars cut through his bottom lip like claw marks, trailing down his chin. The skin is smooth like the scar is a burn rather than a cut and I wonder if that's why he chose the melting mask.

I clench my teeth, then say, "You touch me, and only me."

"Oh shit," Viper says with a dark laugh, gripping the base of his cock. "Sweet little kitty isn't as timid as we thought."

Striker runs his hand down my hair, smoothing my skin, caressing my lower back, trailing fingers over my hip. Then he grips my elbow, like he's silently demanding I stop this insane urge to own Reaper.

Cora shatters, her whimpers filling the room, begging for our attention, but Reaper's eyes never leave mine.

CHAPTER 8

DELILAH

I'VE NEVER BEEN ONE to back down from a fight.

Right now? The way Reaper's dark eyes are cutting through me with such intensity, it feels like my flesh is burning, I want to tuck my tail between my legs and run. But I don't. Even as the tangled vines of jealously grow black thorns and withered buds bloom in my chest, I set my jaw and keep him pinned with my gaze, refusing to back down. His jaw ticks and he lets his eyes drop to my mouth.

We've entered dangerous territory. The way I'm directing this man who obviously doesn't like to be told what he can and cannot do, may just be my undoing. But he doesn't know my will is just as strong as his.

And I do *not* want him touching Cora.

Running his tongue along his bottom lip, his jaw pops, then he says, "I won't touch her." He nods to the three men around us. "But they *all* will touch you. *Everywhere*."

The charged tension in the room snaps just as quickly as it pulled tight between us. My breath rushes out, an electric shiver making my skin prick. Heat floods between my legs, my already dripping core now aching, wanting to be filled even more than before as his words, his *threat*, radiates between my legs, saturating my blood with a primal need.

Cora's whimpers die down, and Breaker leans over, kissing the side of her face as he thrusts, grunting quietly, dragging everyone's attention back to them. A low growl escapes, his forehead dropping to her back as he pumps, his movements becoming jerky as his orgasm crashes through him.

Striker pulls my arm away from Reaper and I look back over at him, letting my body relax.

"You're ballsy," he says with a smirk, "But I don't think you realize what you've just done."

On my other side, Breaker leans up, chest heaving, and smacks Cora lightly on the ass. Pulling out, his thick length gleaming with wetness, he places another kiss on her back before falling to the couch. The front of his black shirt clings to his sculpted chest, damp with sweat, and he pulls it away from his skin. He tugs the material up slightly, his glistening abs on display, pants undone, his slick cock still thick, resting on the open zipper.

He's fucking gorgeous. Strong and masculine.

My eyes snag on black lines inked into his dark skin, hinting at a large tattoo over his abdomen, but hidden under his shirt. When he catches me openly staring, he shoots me a wink, then turns his attention back to Cora, helping her pull herself together. Cora sits upright, pressing her glistening thighs closed, wiping her sweaty hair from her pink cheeks.

Underneath me, I feel Reaper move, his hard length pressing into my back. "Viper, clean our sweet little girl up."

On command, Viper drops to his knees and pulls Cora's thighs open. She gasps out a surprise, but it turns into a throaty groan when Viper's mouth descends on her, lapping at the mess between her thighs.

My pussy throbs at the sight, and like he knows what I need, Striker's fingers slip into me again, driving in so hard I jolt, my eyes never leaving Viper.

"That's it," Breaker praises, cupping the back of Viper's head as it moves between her splayed legs. "Clean up my mess like the dirty boy I know you are."

"Are you ready, Kitten?" Reaper whispers in my ear, his tongue flickering over the sensitive skin. Goose bumps break out over my body, my nipples tightening. "I promised to fill you up with my cum."

Lowering his mouth again, Striker licks my clit, sucking it into his mouth, then letting it go with a slick pop. My belly dips, the sensation like I've just dropped several floors in an elevator making my head spin. His fingers slip in and out, the sound of my arousal making obscene wet sounds. "She's so fucking wet. Her pussy is weeping for you, Reap."

"Good girl," Reaper says, unclasping my bra and letting it fall away. "I want you begging for me."

Striker's fingers slip out and a sharp slap lands on my clit. I bite my lip, my eyes flying to Striker to catch his smirk right when he grasps my wrist, pinning it to Reaper's thigh as he sits back on the couch next to us. My heart thunders as Reaper grips my other arm and drags it behind me, pushing me forward slightly and pinning it to my lower back.

"Breaker come tease this pretty little Kitten," Reaper orders. "We want her begging for my cock."

With a devious smile, Breaker drops to his knees before me. He's so tall that he still looms over me.

"Hi, Tiny Thing," he says, cupping my cheeks before leaning in to place a gentle kiss on my lips, then trailing soft kisses down my jaw to my collarbone.

I throw my head back, soaking up the warm glow he leaves behind. His large hands caress my breasts, pinching my nipples and rolling them, sending a sharp pang to my clit. Lowering his head, he sucks a nipple into his mouth hard, teeth biting almost painfully around the bud. I arch into him, loving the smooth feel of his lips and jaw on my skin, mixing with the harsh bite of his teeth. He nibbles at the hardened bud, then releases me, kissing a line of fire back up to my mouth. With another soft kiss, he backs away, letting his palms rest on my open thighs.

"Hi," I say, when our eyes lock, my chest heating, blood burning through me as I watch him lower his mouth to me and swirl his hot tongue through my folds. I gasp, amazed at how different his mouth feels from Striker's.

Cora's groan makes me look over and our eyes meet as Viper devours her, gripping her thighs to hook her legs over his shoulders. Her hips rock, meeting his mouth, her arms spread out to hold herself upright, fingers curled into the leather cushion.

"Oh my *god*," she whimpers, her voice breaking on the last word. "I'm going to come again."

Everything in me leans forward, Breaker's swirling tongue adding to the clawing craving scratching through me. I want to capture her mouth, suck her plush lips between my teeth and bite down hard. Make her scream louder as she comes this time. The thoughts rush through me, making me even wetter and I hear Breaker groan, lapping at me hungrily. With my hands trapped in their massive grip, I'm unable to move. The realization that I'm trapped, held in place by these powerful men, forced to bend to their will, crashes a wave of pure heated desire through my body. I drop my gaze to watch Breaker lick up my center, his pale eyes moving up to meet mine.

"She likes this," Breaker says, between licks. "Watching her friend get eaten out."

"She's close," Reaper says, his free hand moving around to cup my breast, rolling a peaked bud between his fingers roughly, the material of his gloves sending shivers up my back. "Don't let her come."

That craving snakes through me, coiling tightly up inside until I'm tilting my hips, trying to press Breaker harder to me. The muscles in my legs tighten, my belly fluttering as his mouth takes me higher and higher. Striker leans over to capture my lips and I devour his kiss, the need to wrap my arms around him and pull his hard, warm body against mine, nearly making me want to weep. Right before my orgasm crashes through me, Breaker backs away and Striker breaks our kiss. I growl in frustration, my shoulders tensing in disbelief.

"The fuck," I snarl, my brows knit as Breaker smirks and stands.

"You're going to come on my cock," Reaper says in my ear, releasing my hand.

I reach for my aching clit, but Breaker catches my wrist with a chuckle as Striker pulls me from Reaper's lap.

"Hands and knees," Reaper orders as he stands, turning me until I'm facing the couch.

My body buzzes like a live wire is pressed to my skin, my blood sizzling, making it hard to think beyond one primal craving.

Casting Reaper a look over my shoulder, I lower myself to the soft leather with trembling legs, resting my knees in the center of the seat and leaning forward. Striker moves to the back and grasps my hands, placing them on the back of the couch. My eyes fall to his large hands unbuckling his belt. Striker grips my chin and pulls my face to his. He leans down and brushes a soft kiss to my lips. Behind me, I hear Reaper's belt clinking and his zipper grating down.

"You ready, Princess?" Striker says, releasing me and backing up enough to slide his belt open and pop the button of his pants.

His words from earlier crash through me. With slow movements, he slides his zipper down and frees himself, his large dick springing free, bobbing up to his navel. He grips the root and slides his hand over his shaft, stroking himself. He's just as long and thick as the other's, but he's so hard, the vein running along the underside so prominent; it has to be painful.

Behind me, I feel Reaper's hand grasp my hip. His dick slips over my opening and I let out a low moan, the head slipping into me slightly before moving out.

"Fuck," Reaper hisses. "She likes the sight of your dick. Her pussy is fluttering."

"Naughty Princess," Striker growls. "You like watching me stroke my cock for you?"

Heat floods my pussy, and I clench around the head of Reaper's dick. My head swirls. A primitive need flushes my face and chest, and I grip the back of the couch, angling my hips to accept Reaper. I want him inside me. Moving, thrusting. I want his heat and his cum. *Him.*

"Answer him, Kitten," Reaper warns, inching in even more. His fingers weave into my hair, jerking my head back to expose my throat. "You always answer when we speak to you."

"God, yes," I groan, the breathy sound of my voice unrecognizable. *I'm* unrecognizable. My pants and moans sound like they're coming from a different woman. "Please. Reaper. Striker."

"Better be careful," Striker warns. "Reaper doesn't show mercy to those who beg."

CHAPTER 9

DELILAH

REAPER'S DARK CHUCKLE FILLS my ears right before he slams forward. My arms give from the force, my chest hitting the cool leather couch, and I cry out at the sting of pain. He's huge, my body stretching around him, trying to accept him as he slips in deeper.

"Fuck, she's tight," Reaper growls and pulls back, giving me a slight reprieve.

Striker grips my chin and guides me up, helping me brace myself again. "I warned you, Princess. Reaper doesn't take orders from anyone."

The sting fades as he slides out, then repeats the movement just as brutally, sliding in even deeper than before.

"That's it, Kitten, take all of me," Reaper says. "I'm going to fuck you rough and hard. Just the way I like it."

Reaper pulls back and slams forward, building up a steady, hard pace. A raw hunger slashes through me, cutting up my insides, making a low hiss slip out through gritted teeth. Gripping the edge of the couch back, I adjust my knees, opening wider, his brutal pounding and the stinging stretch making my heart beat frantically, a wildfire of blistering desire turning my blood to lava.

"Good, little Kitten," Reaper growls, yanking my hair to jerk my head back even more, somehow slipping in deeper, harder. This doesn't feel like a giving of pleasure. This feels like rage pouring out of him and into me. "You take my cock so well for such a bratty little girl."

"She needs to be kissed," Striker says, softly petting my head.

He's right. I need something. A kiss, a gentle touch, something other than the carnal desire crashing through me. Other than the vicious driving of Reaper's cock. Other than the tightness in my chest that seems to wrap around my lungs compressing and expanding all at once.

Leaning down, Striker drives his tongue past my lips and I open for him, moaning into his mouth. Savoring his soft touch and the way he takes my kiss gently. Sweetly. Demanding from me in a way that leaves my chest aching. The feel of Reaper moving in so brutally contrasts with Striker's softness. I melt into him, for him, my body loosening for Reaper when Striker cups my jaw and whispers sweet words against my mouth.

You're taking him so well, Princess.

Open wider for him.

Let him in deep.

The punishing grip in my hair yanks my head back further, but this time the ruthless force sends desire through me. I succumb to the almost violent scratching of pleasure. My hips tilt, my body relaxing, pushing back into him harder with each thrust. Silently begging for more. Harder. Faster. *Meaner.* Until I'm caught up in an intense, brutal wave, taking him all the way as I meet his thrusts, needing to be fucked savagely. My inner walls tremble, my release building up higher and higher.

"Fuck," Reaper grates the word. "Yes, Kitten. Suck me in deep into your greedy pussy."

Releasing my lips, Striker steps back and grips his cock, guiding himself to my mouth. I open for him, just like he knew I would. Not just complying with his demand, but wanting him to fill me. He grips my jaw, running the pad of his thumb over my bottom lip.

"Look at you, Princess," he grates. "So beautiful and desperate for me."

"Come here, baby girl," Reaper says, thrusts slowing, snapping my focus on Cora. I feel her arm slip against my sweaty thigh as she sits next to me on the couch.

"What a needy little thing," Reaper says to her, and that green weed of jealousy snakes through my middle. I rip my head to the side to make sure he's not touching her, but my shoulders soften when I see Breaker kissing down her body, sucking her breasts into his mouth, then slipping down further.

"She is a sweet, pretty little thing," Breaker says from between her legs.

"Viper, fuck her mouth," Reaper orders, his thrusts turning slower, but no less brutal. "But be gentle."

A pang of anger needles through my core, the sting spearing up my back from between my legs where he's fucking me. Nothing Reaper is doing to me is gentle.

Striker leans forward and grips my throat, wrapping his long fingers around my neck until I'm forced to focus back on him. He slips the head of his dick over my lips. My tongue flickers out, eagerly tasting the clean masculine pre-cum.

"Do you see what you do to me?" he asks, as I lick his slickness from my lips. "You make my cock so hard, I may lose my mind if I don't come soon."

Reaper slams forward the same moment Striker slips into my mouth, hitting the back of my throat. He holds himself there as I gag, tears spilling down my cheeks. Throwing his head back, he does it again, letting out a rumbling groan, moving his hips to meet with how my body is driving forward with Reaper's thrusts.

"Oh, fuck," Striker grates, his eyes lowering to mine. His grip at my throat tightens as he drives in again, pulling out just long enough for me to suck in air. "Princess, you're heaven. Pure fucking heaven."

Next to us, I hear Cora's choked groan as Viper drives into her mouth. "Oh god," he grates.

"Baby girl, play with Kitten's pussy," Reaper rasps, his breaths coming faster, thrusts turning harder. "Make her come all over my cock."

Reaper's command shoots to my clit. Cora touching me? A grating carnal need snakes up between my legs, growing more wild and desperate. The thought of her...

I let go of the couch, my hand seeking hers. It lands on her shoulder and I move it lower, feeling soft sticky skin and the top of her breast. Warm, small fingers slide around my leg, and I grip her wrist, guiding her to me. I choke on the sensation of her fingers brushing over me until she finds my clit. Her fingers move lower, feeling Reaper slamming into me between her fingers. She drags the wetness back up to my clit, circling roughly, and I can do nothing but return my grip to the couch and hold on.

Reaper growls behind me, the hand in my hair tightens. The groan that tears from my throat sounds primitive, ripping free of some wild creature.

"Oh shit," Striker rasps. "She's about to come."

"Come on my cock, Kitten," Reaper says.

Striker drives in deep, holding himself at my throat. My pussy throbs, my eyes watering, my throat raw and used, but he pulls back just when the need to breathe becomes too much and I suck in air. He does it again, saliva dripping down my chin and pooling on my neck where he's gripped my throat.

It all becomes too much. How Reaper's driving into me so hard, thrusting me forward with a silent hatred. Striker moving in and out of my mouth, his hand at my neck squeezing tightly. Cora's soft moans as Breaker laps at her, mixed with Viper's curses as she sloppily sucks him into her mouth. Her rough, frantic touch between my legs. It builds up higher and higher until I want to fold in on myself. Lower my forehead to the back of the couch and let it consume me. The burning heat slowly spreading through my body, coiling up tightly in my lower belly, tells me that when I break, I'll shatter into a million pieces.

Striker's grip tightens and my eyes squeeze shut. Gripping the couch, I dig my nails into the soft leather as they both thrust forward. My knees slip on the cushion, my breasts hitting the cool leather on back of the couch.

"Fuck," he breathes. "I'm going to come, Princess. I'm going to fill your mouth up so good."

His movements become sloppy, jerky, right before salty heat surges into my mouth. He hits deep and I choke on his cum, gagging on his dick as he slips it in and out, fucking my mouth through his release. Cum spills out between each thrust, gathering between my throat and his hand.

"Swallow it all, Princess," Striker rasps, pulling out. I swallow as much as I can, but the pressure on my neck and the angle Reaper's holding my head makes it difficult. Using two fingers, Striker gathers the cum spilling down my chin and swipes it back into my mouth. "Suck it all off."

Obediently, I close my mouth around his fingers.

Cora's hands stills for a moment as she moans around Viper's dick, but then I hear choked cries mixed with raw, throaty grunts, and her hand moves again.

"Oh god," I whimper, when Striker's fingers leave my mouth, feeling it all building so high, I think I may break in all the wrong ways. Every nerve ending is lit too bright. My body too alive with electricity. Everything is too intense. Too many hands. Too many sensations. "Oh, god. Oh, god."

"That's right," Reaper growls. "We're your fucking gods tonight."

"Come for him, Princess," Striker says, squeezing my throat and petting my hair like I'm something precious. Something breakable. And right now, I think I may be. "You're so beautiful with my cum spilling from your mouth. Imagine how gorgeous you'll be with Reaper's cum filling your tight pussy."

"Come on, Kitten," Reaper grates. "Let go."

Like my body just needed his command, everything breaks away all at once. My scream cuts through the room, pure pleasure ripping from me, out of me, my walls clenching down on Reaper so tight he shouts a curse. The sharp bite of teeth cuts into my shoulder. Reaper's hand lands next to mine on the couch's back. The world blacks out, my pulse thumping in my ears, blocking out all other sounds before they come crashing back in. My arms give and I fall forward, the motion causing Striker's grip to cut off air before he lets go.

Gripping the back of the couch, Reaper's throaty growl grows quiet as heat floods me. His hips jerk wildly. He drives in deep, once, twice, filling me up, his heat slipping out, coating my inner thighs as he pumps me full.

Then silence.

For a moment, it's just heavy breathing, and then the world slowly comes back into focus. My eyes land on Reaper's large, gloved hand that's somehow moved over mine.

"You're going to remember the way I felt deep in you," he whispers against my ear, pressing his hips to my ass, holding his cum in me where it pulses deep inside my core. "At night when you're cursing my name, you'll remember how much you wanted my cum in you."

CHAPTER 10

DELILAH

T HE SINGLE BEAM OF light streaming in through the slit
in the heavy curtains paints a bright line across the blankets. I groan, wincing at the tender ache between my legs, and
roll to look at the clock on the nightstand. The shiny metallic
hands tell me it's well past noon.

Dammit.

I lurch upright in the bed, my head swimming. My hand
moves to my forehead, the pounding throbbing behind my eyes
making me regret the several bottles of champagne Cora and I
shared after the men left.

The night flashes through my mind and heat builds in
my belly, right as a flood of panic fills my chest, making it feel

tight. I squeeze my eyes shut, trying to process it all. So much happened. For so long. Anxiety needles at my middle, but I push it away, pressing my fingers to my lips, remembering Cora's soft kisses. With a deep breath, the lingering feeling of her fingers on me charges a bolt of desire to my clit, and I press my thighs together.

Shit.

I let her kiss me.

I let him come in me.

Them, Delilah. I let Striker come in my mouth.

My head drops to my hands. I was so reckless. So *unlike* me. As wonderful as it would be to rub Dave's face in my crazy behavior last night, let him squirm at the idea that not only another man wanted me, but *several*, no one can find out.

I glance around the room, taking in the disaster we made last night. Champagne bottles scatter the floor. My costume and what's left of my fishnets lay next to the window and I can almost hear Cora's high-pitched laughter as I stripped for her before the rest of the night goes black. Shit. I barely even remember coming up here, so it's impossible to know what sort of ruckus we caused.

Fragments of memories filter back. I faintly remember demanding the top floor suite after we left the club, the poor girl at the desk handing me the room access codes with a trembling hand. With that type of behavior out in public, it's a wonder we made it back to the room without someone notifying my father that his daughter was in one of the club's private rooms, partying with four men, then causing a scene in the lobby.

Then again, maybe they figured I deserved to be a little wild considering how tight a rope he's had on me my entire life. Or maybe they didn't want to sound the alarm after they saw the two of us stagger from the private room with costumes askew, stockings either gone or ripped, each clutching a champagne bottle and crystal flutes, stumbling down the hall to the elevators once I got our room code.

"You okay?"

I lock onto Cora's bright green eyes peering up at me from under the blankets. Black streaks mar her face and her green eye shadow and red lipstick are long gone. My shoulders sag. I know I must look similar. Completely and utterly destroyed from being used by four men.

I slip back down into the bed, turning on my side to face her. We should already be up and at the meeting my father scheduled for early this morning, but he's going to have to wait until we pull ourselves together. The worried expression on her face tells me we need to talk through what we did last night. And not just what we did with the guys, but with each other. Even in all our drunken nights and with how wild Cora's been, we've never gone *this* far. What we did last night was extreme by both our standards.

"Regrets?" she asks, biting her bottom lip.

I'm not sure if she means regrets from us kissing or the entire night.

She scans my face like she's trying to read me. Gauge my answer before I can speak.

Do I have regrets?

My gaze falls over her shoulder to the curtains and the beam of light. Last night, Reaper pulled out of me, and left the room. The other three at least had the decency to clean us up a little and sit for a minute before giving us each a parting kiss. I may not be wise in the ways of sexual encounters, and I know that was a one-night thing, but Reaper's sudden departure left me feeling dark. Used. Empty.

Blinking away the thoughts, I plaster a grin on my face. "That was crazy."

She giggles, covering her mouth with the blanket, muffling the girlish sound. Loving the mischievous sparkle in her eyes, my mind wanders back to last night.

Cora tucks the blanket under her chin. "You kiss really well," she whispers.

Our eyes meet, my belly fluttering with a strange heat. Her lip quirks and we both break out into laughter, gripping the blankets to pull them over our heads.

"So do you," I say, keeping my voice low. Under the dark blankets, I can barely make out her freckled cheeks, but now they grow red when she's flustered. "Do you have regrets?"

She blows out a breath and I think of Striker's warm mouth on my neck. "No," she whispers after a moment. "I would totally do that again and more."

"Cora!" I laugh, using my toe to nudge her shin.

"And you wouldn't?" Her brow lifts. "Naughty Kitten."

Reaper's words ring in my head, and my smile falls, my laughter fading.

"I can't believe—" Cora's words get cut off when we hear the suite door closing with a loud thud.

Panic zips through me, and I throw the blankets back, clutching them to my chest as I sit upright. It's at this moment that I realize I'm naked.

"Delilah?" a gruff voice barks out and my shoulders lower. "Cora?"

"In here," Cora calls, lifting the blankets to look at her body, as if to make sure she's really naked.

When our gazes lock, she puffs out a breath, her eyes wide. I don't think we did anything else when we got back to the room, at least not that I remember. Even so, this looks bad. But honestly, I'd rather my father think Cora and I fucked last night than know about the four men we actually did.

My father's advisor appears in the suite's bedroom doorway, his dark eyes falling over us huddled in the bed. This alone isn't unusual. We've shared a bed plenty of nights over the years, but our messy state and knotted hair turns his expression dour.

Not usually one to react to much of anything, Clyde lifts a single dark brow and enters the room, tossing two garment bags on the armchair by the bathroom. Gripping the velvet curtains, he pulls them wide open and Cora and I both cover our eyes and groan at the sudden flash of sunlight.

"You two made quite an impression on *someone* last night," he says, motioning to someone in the doorway. "They sent gifts."

The hotel's concierge, the only one Clyde would allow to witness his precious girls in this state, pushes in a food cart, covered with several dishes. Not making eye contact, and decidedly *not* looking at the state of the room, he parks the cart next to the heavy wooden table and chairs near the windows and retreats, returning a few moments later with two massive bouquets of coral colored roses and burgundy dahlias so dark they look nearly black.

Cora gasps at my side and throws the covers back, not caring about her nakedness as she shoots from the bed, running toward the massive bouquets. The concierge blinks, averting his eyes. He gives a subtle nod to Clyde and backs out of the room gracefully.

"Jesus, girl," Clyde says, his brown eyes rolling to the ceiling. "Have some tact."

"It wasn't tact that got us these flowers," she tells him, lifting a rose from the vase and bringing it to her nose.

Clyde's focus falls on me and his brow raises.

"Don't worry," I tell him, wrapping the sheet around my chest, eyeing the cart laden with food. When I stand, the room sways slightly, and my legs tremble. A deep ache in my core sends a reminder to my belly with a flutter. My eyes catch on my reflection in the mirror across the room and my stomach sinks. My black hair's a mess from the many hands in it last night. The black eyeliner runs in streaks down my cheeks. Fuck. I look ravaged. I glance back at Clyde. "We didn't cause a stir."

Liar. I'm going to have to thank the staff from last night discreetly.

When I step up to the cart, Clyde's stern eyes assess me and when his focus snaps to my neck, I reach up, feeling the sensitive skin.

His shoulder's tense, eyes turning deadly. "Delly?"

Fuck. There must be bruises. I cup my neck, averting my eyes. "I'm fine."

I can only imagine what he's thinking. The way his lips press into a thin line and the hard, gritting set of his jaw tells me he's probably wondering which one of his soldiers my father will want to send to kill whoever I was with last night.

I chuckle, thinking of the army he'd have to send to deal with those big boys.

"I'm a big girl," I remind him. Popping a grape into my mouth, I gesture to the garment bags. "For our meeting?"

"Which you missed this morning." Clyde's eyes drag down to my feet, then dart over to my costume on the floor. "Your father rescheduled for the afternoon."

"Lucky us," I say, loading up a plate with more fruit.

Clyde narrows his eyes at my remark, and turns to address Cora, but his shoulders drop when he sees she's still naked as she admires the flowers. Honestly, I'm not sure what I think about the men's gifts. It feels like a sweet gesture but also, like a "thanks for letting me come in you, it was fun," move that leaves me feeling a little slimy. Cora obviously doesn't share my thoughts, so maybe I'm over-reacting. I'm not exactly schooled in the art of one-night stands.

Just the art of hiding my father's power and greed.

"Fuck, girl, put some clothes on," he tells Cora, then turns back to me. "Who are the flowers from, Delly?"

Cora chuckles.

"Did Daddy say if the client signed the forms?" I ask, biting into more fruit and smiling sweetly.

Clearly refusing to take the bait and the subject change, Clyde steps closer, his stern features growing harder. "Is there a mess that needs tidying?"

My bark of laughter makes Clyde's lip curl. "Our night was hardly that adventurous," I tell him.

Cora opens her mouth but I shoot her a look. She clamps it shut, sauntering to the food cart, eating bacon off the tray, her lush breasts on full display. The distinct outline of finger shaped bruises scatter her outer thighs, but I hope Clyde doesn't notice. He'd go completely ape-shit. Where my father's love is protective, Clyde's is outright dangerous.

Clyde glances at her, then back at me. I know he's just trying to protect us, mostly from my father. He knows more than anyone how Rune overreacts to any threat to me or Cora. We're his jewels. His future. His most precious investment.

I take in Clyde's three-piece suit, the grays peppering his temples, and the lines feathering his dark skin around his brown eyes. He's been with my father since the beginning. The only person on this entire planet my father trusts with his life. And mine. The things Clyde has done to protect this family...

I don't even want to think about it.

Even though I've been sheltered from the violent aspects of my father's business, I know Clyde's killed people. Many people. He wouldn't blink if Rune decided to go after the men Cora and I had fun with last night, simply because my father doesn't like the thought of me being tainted.

I swallow my irritation. This is why it's important to make sure I keep our night a secret. Those men were just looking for fun. That's it. They don't need a mildly psychotic father figure biting at their heels after we willingly spent the evening with them. Those four did nothing wrong.

"No, Clyde," I tell him, growing serious, "there's nothing to clean up."

He nods, seemingly satisfied with my answer.

"You know your father doesn't like to be left waiting," Clyde says as I sit at the table with my plate.

Unease grips my belly and my gaze slips to Cora. She grimaces and leaves the room, shutting the bathroom door behind her.

Lucky. How I wish I could slip away so easily.

"I know," I tell him, remembering Breaker giving me a similar warning about Reaper. "Tell Daddy that Cora and I will be with him soon."

CHAPTER 11

CORA

WHEN LIFE GIVES YOU lemons, make lemonade.

Or, in my case, lemon creme pie. Everyone loves lemon cream pie. At least I know Rune does. That's why when he took me in when I was only ten years old, I remade myself. Molded my body and mind to fit his life. I had no choice.

It was I fit in or I died like my parents.

"Is it possible?" Rune asks, his blue eyes darting between me and Delly. We've reassured him several times already that we've covered his tracks, but I think he's growing more paranoid in his old age.

Delly and I flank either side of him at his massive boardroom table where he sits at the head, the large windows framing him like he's a god. We've spent the last hour here in this room, listing the reasons he shouldn't worry, but it's not working. He's tense today, no doubt because of this merger. I hate it when he gets this way. It means only one thing.

My eyes move to Delilah across the table. She cleaned up nicely, but I know she still feels like shit. Just like me. She masked her emotions about last night, but she's always been good at that. Coming across as unfeeling and callous. But I know her. She's anything but.

I saw her wince as she got ready, pulling on her pencil skirt after her shower. Reaper had been rough, fucking her like he hated her. As she covered up the faint bruises around her neck from Striker's brutal grip, I wondered if she regretted last night.

I don't. I've been with two men before, but never four. And never a woman. Hell, I didn't even know I wanted to be with a woman until Delly kissed me. No, not just any woman. Her specifically. My friend that's been more like a sister to me over the last fifteen years of our lives. But sisters don't kiss and they certainly don't slip fingers between their sister's legs.

When her lips met mine, it felt like I'd been shoved off a cliff. It was forbidden. The two of us. But it felt so right. So...

Perfect.

"Well?" Rune asks gruffly, and I realize he's talking to me.

Smiling sweetly, I reach across the table, and I curl my fingers around his large hand. A hint of darkness passes over his features at my touch, but he flips his palm up and squeezes my hand. His hard edges always soften with my touch. Rune's used my softness, my sweetness, over the years to keep himself calm. To unravel the dangerous rage that lives inside him, leaving him pliable. Malleable. Easy to mold like I was for him.

And he likes it when I gently accept his roughness. He always has the times he's shoved his dick into my mouth, my moans, the way my hand slips between my thighs, turning his hard, mean touch into soft praises and light pets for the girl that represents everything he fears.

He's not a complete monster. He didn't come to me until I was of age, though he did always look at me differently. But, I understand what I am. I am the daughter of his enemies. The child of the two people who betrayed him. I'm sin and betrayal. The receiver of his punishing resentment.

I learned quickly that if I acted scared and timid, crying over his advances, he'd turn meaner. That's why I had to remake myself. Turning my sour fear into the sweetness he could savor. Something he would like to possess, not something he'd abuse and abandon. That first time, when he left me choking on my blood after he hit me over and over, his cum mixing with the metallic tang on my tongue, I decided that he wouldn't hurt me again.

Rune Gavin hates weakness and I'm not weak.

And he didn't hurt me again. Not when I went to him and offered my body for him to use. At least not too badly. Not enough to leave marks. Although, there are still times when he fucks my mouth, that I've seen such hatred from him, it feels like my insides are shriveling up, any love I had hoped had grown over the years dying as he slaps my cheeks and comes in my mouth.

Even though I'm under his protection, I'm not his blood. Traitor blood runs in my veins, so it's understandable he hates me as much as he says he loves me. My parents killed his wife. But I was just an innocent girl caught in a war so he took me in and raised me like his own.

Until he stopped looking at me as his daughter and more like the woman who tore his life apart.

He unravels our fingers and straightens his tie; the movement reminding me of the many times he's loosened it before taking me.

"Yes, Papa," I tell him, my gut churning a little at the name he insists I call him, even when he's using me for his pleasure. *Sick fuck.* Maybe I hate him a little bit too. "You are safe. You know we'll always protect you."

Delly's eyes darken as she watches my hand move back to my lap. She doesn't know. She can't know. It would destroy her to discover what her father's really like and I can't have that.

After last night, after feeling her sweet kiss and the way she came under my touch, I know if Delilah falls, I'll crumble with her.

"The merger money trail is all anyone will find," she says, glancing at her phone as it vibrates with an incoming message. "Even if they dig, all anyone will see is that Rune Corporations bought out Snyder, Inc. and we now own the entire chain of hotels along the west coast."

Rune nods, watching as she unlocks her phone to read the message. Her brows furrow and her blue eyes flash up to mine. Something in her expression sends dread spiraling through me, settling in my already churning gut.

"Alright then," Rune says and stands from the table.

Returning my focus back to Rune, I admire his sleek charcoal suit and the waves of black hair peppered with gray. He's let his hair grow out, which makes his handsome face look younger than he really is. He's not tall, but he feels large. His presence, the essence of him, larger than life, eating up every inch of space. His hand smooths down the front of his suit, over his trim abdomen, tugging at the jacket.

I'm glad he's not fat and round, like most men in the business. It would make choking on his attentions harder to stomach.

His stark blue eyes, just like Delly's, fall on me, making my belly flutter with a mixture of excitement and something else, something I refuse to name, because if I do, I'll splinter into a million particles and dissolve into nothing.

"Cora, sweetie," he says, running his hand over my cheek, "bring the details to my office this afternoon."

With a smile, I stand along with Delly and gather my phone and the file with the merger reports, feeling my insides crack, knowing what will happen when I go to his office. "Will do, Papa."

***

"Who was the text from?" I ask when we've reached the large lobby at the entrance to the corporate offices. Late afternoon sun shines on the gray, glossy marble floors, yellow light pouring in from the floor to ceiling windows that cover the entire front of the skyscraper.

The lobby is empty, except for the two receptionists behind the information desk and a few security personnel. Being a Saturday, the offices above are almost completely empty since few people like to work weekends.

"It's nothing," she says, adjusting the strap of her bag on her shoulder. A shadow passes over her face, and I have a sudden urge to hug her.

Kiss her.

Shit.

This is going to be a problem.

"Fucking hell," she growls, her gaze cutting over to the elevators lining the far wall. I follow her eyes and my stomach lurches, plummeting to my feet.

"Goddammit," I agree.

Stalking toward us, all expensive suit and white teeth, is Zane, the man directly under Rune. Arrogance leaks from him, filling the entire bottom floor with its stench. Money, power, greed. That is Zane Devin.

When Delly married that twat Dave last year, Zane nearly had a brain aneurysm. He's obsessed with Delilah and believes that because Rune trusts him enough to position him right under him, he's somehow entitled to Delilah. A good fifteen years older than us both, he isn't bad looking, so it wouldn't be a terrible thing if her father insisted. Zane is tall, with blonde hair and hazel eyes. He's probably selfish in bed, though, which would never do for a woman like Delly. She's out of his league and he knows it, even if he'll never admit it. He'd rather possess her, force her to submit by any means necessary than actually be worthy of her.

Actually, I think he'd like it if her father forced her to marry him.

I know he'd settle for me, but Delly is the prize mare. She's perfect. Intelligent, graceful, rich. The daughter of Rune Gavin and so gorgeous it makes any man want to drop to his knees to please her. The opposite of me, she's the perfect trophy. Where I'm soft and light, all round curves with a fiery temper and wild streak, she's dark, sleek, almost panther-like in her perfection. Calm and collected.

Except last night.

My lip curls in amusement at the thought of Zane seeing her the way she was last night—obediently taking every inch, submitting to every filthy demand. Leaking cum and choking on several men's dicks. A shiver passes through me. I'd like to see her like that again. So out of control and wanton. Carefully deconstructed and breaking apart under my touch. I loved that it was my hand coated in her wet heat. *My* fingers playing with her sensitive clit, helping to push her over the edge.

"Dammit," she grumbles, taking a step back toward the doors at our backs. "I don't have it in me today."

"Because you had so much in you last night?"

She glares at my smirk before looking around. When she spots Rune exiting the elevators, she squares her shoulders and grabs my hand in a tight grip. Feeling the slick sickness combined with the confusing pleasure returning to my gut, knowing I have to be near Rune again, I resist the urge to pull away and follow her. She wants to avoid Zane, and I don't blame her, but he'll be more subdued with her father around.

"Delilah," Zane calls, pivoting to follow us across the space.

His thundering voice makes a few people pause, and when they see Zane, several people head for the front door. God, if only we could run away too.

Rune spots us right before his eyes land on Zane at our backs. He knows what Zane craves and I can practically see his hackles rise as he moves toward us with Clyde at his heels, his two bodyguards in tow. The rest of the people lingering in the lobby scatter like the roaches they are. You can't work in this building and not know what Rune Gavin is. Delly and I were born into this. We don't have a choice. They, on the other hand, choose to work for a criminal.

Still holding my hand, she drags me forward, our heels clacking loudly in the suddenly nearly empty space.

"Delly," Zane says from behind us, making her turn and release my hand. Even though we've lost that physical connection, I can still feel her annoyance.

"What can I help you with, Mr. Devin?" she asks sweetly, and I suppress a chuckle

If he only knew the things she'd said about him. An annoying hyena always lapping at her heels. She'd once said he was like a starving dog, rooting around for scraps of her attention. She doesn't know that he's really a cunning chameleon, ready to change his colors the second the need calls for it.

Zane leans in, kissing her cheek lightly. "Are we still on for dinner?" he asks, and I can practically see his jaw clench as he reins in his naturally ruthless demeanor to ask rather than demand. Little does he know she enjoyed being ordered around.

"Dinner?" she asks, her pleading eyes landing on Rune.

"Not tonight," Rune tells Zane, his eyes darting to the front of the building. Something dark flickers over his features and he leans into Clyde, whispering in his ear. With a curt nod, Clyde moves to the nearest soldier Rune keeps at all times to watch his back in public, saying something as he motions to the doors.

Zane seems to sense her father's irritation and sudden mood change and backs down, but his teeth still flash when he smiles. "Another night then," he says as he backs away, briefly glancing over his shoulder to the door, where a security guard positioned himself before he walks away.

Delilah's shoulders relax as she watches him retreat, but stiffen again as she digs her phone from her suit jacket, reading the screen.

"What's wrong, Delly?" I ask, focusing on her puzzled expression, ignoring the ping of the elevator behind us, just glad that Zane is gone.

She holds up the phone, letting me read the screen.

UNKNOWN: "I SHALL NEVER BE WEAK NOR BE AS COMMON AS OTHER MEN."

I open my mouth to ask what the fuck that's supposed to mean when the world explodes.

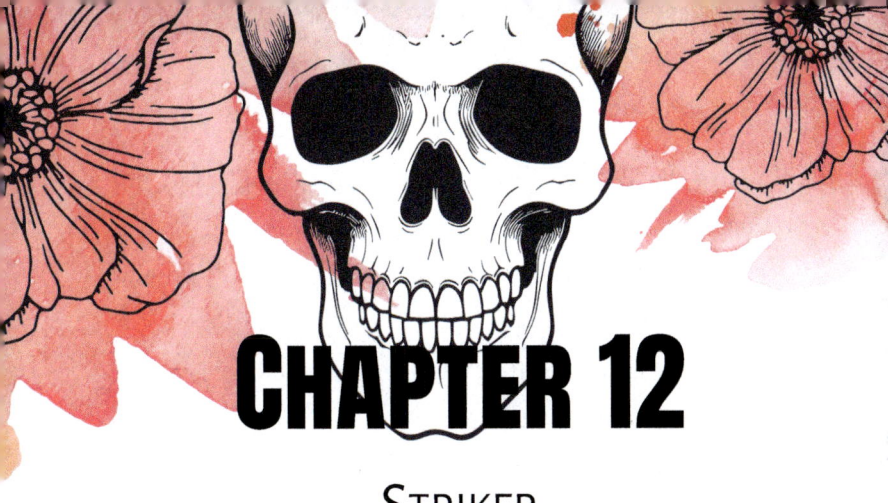

CHAPTER 12

STRIKER

IT'S FUCKING BOILING INSIDE the work van that we parked a few spaces down from the building. Even with the passenger window open, it feels like an oven inside. The slightly burning smell of hot asphalt mixes with the cleaning chemicals in the van, the small made up cleaning supply company acting as our cover. We rarely have to wait so long, but our target was late.

I pull the fabric of my black uniform shirt away from my body. It sticks to my lower back; the sweat pooled there making me itch. I fucking hate being sweaty.

That intense need to be clean should have been removed long ago along with any need for comfort at the school, but it's clung to me all these years. I guess some things can't be beaten out of a man.

Like the need I felt last night as it scraped down my spine and settled in my gut.

"Five more minutes," Breaker says, pulling his glove back to look at his watch.

It's so hot in here that he's pulled his mask up, revealing his high cheekbones and powerful jaw. There is a part of me that's always envied how pretty he is. As kids, anyone who glanced his way knew he was going to grow into a good-looking man.

My insides squirm, remembering last night. We've shared a lot of women over the years. Hell, Reaper and I have grown used to watching Viper suck Breaker's cock. Even grown a little excited seeing how Breaker strokes Viper letting him come in his hand, but with all the crazy shit we've done, fuck, all the kinky ass shit we've done around one another, I'd never felt such heat flare through me at the sight of Viper pleasuring Breaker before.

Last night felt... different. Intense in ways I don't think any of us have experienced before.

And I think it was because of them.

The pretty princess and the poisonous vixen.

"You're floating," Reaper snaps, bringing my mind back to the present as he waves his hand in my face. "Focus, Striker, I need you focused."

"Yes, sir." I nod, shifting on the bench lining the wall of the van. He's the one who can bring me back. Always.

"Stop floating," he says, his eyes never leaving the front window and the building a few spots down from where we parked the van.

That's what he always used to say to me when things got a tad too hard and my mind would drift. Stop floating. Stop and focus. Breathe, Striker. What do you smell?

Sweet floral perfume and a honey cunt.

What do you taste?

The sharp flavor of champagne and the salty sweat on her skin.

What do you hear?

Vixen's soft cries of pleasure and the desperate moans of a needy princess.

"Strike?" I glance up and find Viper's eyes.

Yeah. I'm distracted.

He gives me a slight nod, letting me know he understands. I'm glad I'm not the only one. But then, Viper and I have always had an understanding. Reaper says we're the sensitive ones in our group. Like that's a negative thing. A mark against us for having held on to a sliver of our humanity after the school tried to extract every ounce from us. I say it keeps us grounded.

At least most of the time.

Sometimes, when things get too hard, times I don't even notice, my mind floats away.

"Get ready," Reaper says, snapping me back.

My eyes meet Viper's again. He's on edge as much as I am. His skin looks a little paler than usual today and he's gone yet another day without shaving, telling me he's struggling as much as me. Viper enjoys being clean cut. Prides himself on his all-American good looks and sleek auburn hair. Never mind, he's a fucking Scotsman, but you'd never be able to tell. The school ironed out any accents we had long ago, removing any trace of our heritage until we were nothing but skilled killers. Trackers. Hunters.

Mercenaries available for hire and nothing more.

"We go in ten," Reaper says, eyes still locked on the building. Part of me knows he's looking for her, and a wave of jealousy hits me out of nowhere.

Fuck.

I knew last night was a bad idea. But Reaper insisted. He's the one who planned the night. I think he likes the idea of having tainted them with our sickness. Marking them. I think he likes the idea a little too much.

One thing we learned early in our training was to never get involved with a target. Go in, gather intel, leave unnoticed. Touch nothing. Be ghosts. Invisible. But fuck, we touched. We fed off them, devoured them, and I think maybe, just maybe, may have claimed them.

She did. My Princess. I think she claimed a piece of me. Maybe she claimed part of Reaper too, with the way he's been acting. I don't think he slept much last night after we returned to the house. I know for a fact Breaker and Viper didn't.

When Reaper retreated to hide out in his room, I remained downstairs with Breaker and Viper and watched as Viper sucked Breaker off. They like an audience and I enjoy watching. It's part of why we all work so well together. Reaper commands, we follow. The first time he ordered Viper to take out Breaker's cock and guide it to the wet, waiting cunt that was spread open for us all, he knew what he was doing.

Reaper just knows things, and I think he knows my secret desires as well. There was a part of me that wanted to pull Viper to me. Let him sink my cock deep into his mouth like he was with Breaker. Swallow my cum as I exploded into his mouth. Let Breaker kiss my thighs and run his hands over my chest and then lower.

I thought about taking out my cock and stroking it as I watched the two, but I was scared it would act as an invitation. Scared maybe I wouldn't stop Breaker if he reached for me to help me stroke myself like he does with Viper. Worried maybe I wouldn't stop Viper either if he crawled over and offered his mouth.

So, I sat there and watched, holding back. Wondering if his mouth was as warm as hers. If he was as rough in his desire to see me break as she was or if he'd be as gentle as he seems with Breaker. It wasn't until they left, and I heard Viper's harsh groans from his room that I finally freed myself and fucked my hand, the sounds from the other room, and images of her—of them—fueling me until I exploded into my palm.

When my breathing calmed, I noticed Reaper in the doorway, watching me. Eating up the sight of me. He's always liked watching us fuck or touch ourselves. He enjoys being watched too. I've never analyzed what it means. We all just sort of fell into this together after one insane night and we never stopped.

Last night, as his eyes slipped over me, I considered asking him if he wanted a taste, but then he left, leaving me wondering if he knew. Not just that I fantasized about the girl's mouths, their pretty pink cunts, but of Viper. Of Breaker.

Today... when he looks at me, I can tell he knows my secret, and I think I'm a little relieved. Maybe I don't have to hide it anymore out of fear. Maybe I'm tired of denying it too.

"Fuck, yeah," Breaker says, snapping me brutally out of my mind. I was floating again.

Breaker's buzzing energy fills the van, making the air crack with electricity. Rolling his head, building himself up for what comes next, he lowers his mask and black goggles, then stomps his boots. "You ready, boys?"

"Hold it," Reaper says, "When we go in, keep it tight. I don't want too many casualties."

"We got our orders," Viper says, his muscles tensing, getting prepared. "We know what to do, Reap."

Reaper's jaw clenches. He's been uncharacteristically tense today. His dark, almost black eyes seem more intense than usual. On extraction days, he's usually calm, collected, so in charge of the mission, himself, and us, that all that misplaced energy, all that lack of focus when we're between jobs, flees and he's cool and centered.

Today, though, his entire body is tightly wound, ready to explode at the slightest provocation. When he gets like this, it means one thing.

Something, or someone, has him primed.

I watch as he absently pulls the single strand of black hair he's holding between his thumb and forefinger. I wonder if he knows that we've noticed. How he's kept the single long black hair wrapped around his pinky finger since we left the girls in that club. How he'd plucked it from the glove he'd been wearing and wrapped it around and around his finger, over and over as Breaker drove us back to the house last night. And when it broke into two long strands, he cursed, spitting out the single vulgar word with such rage we all had looked at one another, knowing that whatever he'd thought he had taken from her was really the other way around.

She planted something in him. Or maybe took something from him instead, and I worry about what will happen when he demands she give it back.

We've worked too hard, planned for too long, for something as mild as feelings to stop us. We have this one chance and we're taking it.

We may never again have this chance to pay Rune Gavin back for what he took from us.

Reaper's jerky movement makes me glance in his direction. Angrily, he tosses her black hair to the floor of the van, his eyes homing in on the building. Maybe he doesn't need that single piece of hair anymore because he knows he's about to have it all in his grasp.

Reap runs his fingers through his black hair, making slick strands fall into his eyes. He keeps it shaved at the sides and slicked back over his head. The scars over his lip twitch as he moves his gaze back to the glass fronted building that holds our target. He looks like a Viking, the unhinged gleam in his eyes letting us know he's ready for battle.

Digging into his pocket, he retrieves the burner phone he's used to set this mission up, tapping at the screen. He then tosses it to the floor and slams it with his boot. The loud thud and sharp crack makes Viper's brow quirk. Kicking the pieces of the phone away, Reaper pulls his gloves on and clenches his jaw.

"We go in and extract the package," Breaker says, his eyes flashing to me. He senses it, too.

Reaper is locked and loaded.

We all gear up, pulling on our ski masks and dark glasses, checking our weapons, yet again. Breaker goes through his ritual of patting his gear and crossing himself. Viper watches his routine, and when Breaker's done, rolls his eyes, flexing his fingers one at a time, adjusting his grip on his weapon and lowers his head. I pat the bag around my chest and roll my shoulders, waiting for Reap's order.

"Not just her," Reaper says, pulling his balaclava over his head and adjusting the thick glasses over his eyes. "I want them both."

CHAPTER 13

Delilah

A DEAFENING BOOM FILLS the lobby, and instinctively I drop my bag and fall into a crouch, curling into myself with my arms over my head. A piercing scream rings in my pulsing ears. My father's arm wraps over my shoulder as Cora falls to her knees by my side, her hand gripping my shirt. I grab her arm and drag her to me as my father's other arm tugs her to his chest. The screaming continues, and I realize it's coming from the receptionist's desk behind me.

Someone yells something incoherent and then two sharp claps of gunshots echo through the air. Cora's scream vibrates through me as I wrap my arm around her waist, trying to fold myself over her. Looking up, I see a man dressed in black military-like garb, his back to us, pointing a gun at one of my father's bodyguards. The guard, Manuel, raises his weapon and I open my mouth to tell him to stop, when a shot breaks out and red blooms on the center of his forehead. His knees buckle and my father's longtime security guard crumbles to the floor.

"Go, go!" the second security guard screams, stepping between us crouched on the floor and the man with the gun at the entrance. He motions for us to stand, trying to direct us to the back. "Get the fuck out!"

Less than a second later, three more black-clad soldiers rush through the glass doors, bursting into the lobby with weapons held up. Another rapid succession—*pop, pop, pop*—and the guard in front of us falls. Wet heat splashes across my face and arms. Cora screams again as Clyde hooks an arm around my waist and drags me up to my feet, telling me to *run.*

To move. To get the fuck out.

My heel slips off, and I grip Cora even tighter, pulling her along as Clyde shoves me away, toward the back of the lobby.

"Fuck," Cora chokes on a sob, standing upright trying to move with me, but her foot slips and she falls to her hands and knees.

"Nobody move!" another male screams.

The women behind the reception counter scream, cowering behind the counter with arms up. *Please have hit the emergency call button*, I think as I freeze in place, my gaze flickering around the room, catching on the two security personnel with raised weapons but Clyde steps in front of Cora and me, blocking us from the men weaving through the entrance.

"Weapons down! That's good, boys. Drop 'em. Kick it away!"

"Everyone on the floor!" Another man orders and my blood chills.

Clyde motions for me to get down. My foot slips on something warm and wet and I look down. Red pours from the guard in front of Clyde, running into the thin grout lines and pooling at our feet. Cora looks down at the shiny floor at the same time and sees her palms and knees smeared with red. Her eyes meet mine, the sparkling green bright with terror as she wipes the blood on her thighs.

"Down!" one of them shouts again and I drop to my knees, putting my hands behind my head. A wave of pure fear chills my blood, seizing the air in my lungs. Cora whimpers, following suit. Every instinct in me wants to pull her to me, plaster her to my chest, so she's not scared, but dread pins me in place, and I'm unable to move.

"Rune Gavin," a man calls. The harsh voice reverberates through my bones, almost violently with its demand to be answered.

My father steps forward, but I grip his hand, trying to pull him back. "Daddy, no!"

"I said on your knees," the man hisses, sending a shiver through me. Goose bumps breakout on the back of my neck.

My father yanks his arm from my grasp in rage. "I don't kneel for anyone!" he shouts, refusing to move.

"Daddy," I plead, hoping he'll hear the fear in my voice, but I know it won't matter.

My father doesn't back down.

"There he is," the man says and I see a flash of black as he steps into my view, but it disappears as my father slides in next to Clyde, creating a wall between Cora and me, and the men with weapons.

Fear slithers down my spine.

No, no, no. It's happening again.

Images I locked away threaten to break free.

Growing up, I heard the vague whispers of turf wars. Of other men in the business getting shot in the street, climbing from their cars or having a sudden heart attack in the bed of their mistress. But it all seemed like movie stuff. Something that happened outside the realm of reality.

Until the day someone shot my mother, and it was suddenly very real as I placed my small hands over the bleeding wound.

Cora's panicked whimper centers me and I pull her closer. I scan the lobby, looking for an escape, and my eyes stop on the emergency exit by the elevators. My stomach churns, the realization if we run, we'll get shot before we make it more than a few steps, making my arms tingle with fear.

"No one move!" the man screams in warning.

Shifting, I see the younger receptionist freeze.

"I don't want to shoot you, little girl."

My jaw clenches at the voice, something niggling at the back of my brain.

"What do you want?" Rune barks out, rage spilling from him in waves.

"Something to replace what you stole."

"The fuck are you talking about?" Rune spits out.

"Rune," Clyde warns from his side as his hand reaches behind him, under his coat.

"No, no, Mr. Harlow," the man says, "You don't want to do that."

His hand freezes. Biting my lip, I debate reaching for Clyde's gun, but I know I'm not fast enough. I'm a fucking accountant, not a goddamned gunslinger. Cora seems to sense my thought, and she shakes her head subtly.

"I said knees," the man says. His voice grows louder, and I hear the heavy thud of boots hitting the marble floor as he gets closer, but Clyde and my father's large frames block Cora and me from the soldiers.

"Who do you work for?" Rune asks. "Who sent you?"

"Get down!" one man screams, sending terror churning through my gut and I flinch.

"On your knees, you fucking vile sack of shit," the first man growls. My jaw clenches at the way he spits out the words with such venom.

I move my arms back up behind my head as a large, black gloved hand lands on my father's shoulder, pressing down hard. My father's knees buckle under the pressure and fiery rage bursts through me. How fucking dare these men come in here and force Rune to his knees? Put a gun in his face and threaten him? Rage blisters my insides and I drop my hands, looking up.

My eyes lock on the mask of the man forcing my father to kneel, and my breath freezes in my lungs.

A smirking skull, the jaw melting away, stares back.

My mouth opens, the world tilting sideways.

Cora's choked sob makes bile rise in my throat. "Oh my god," she whispers. "Fuck. Fuck."

My arms snake around my middle, like this will still the bile churning in my stomach.

Using his free hand, Reaper lowers his black glasses and those intense, black-as-night eyes bore into me. Under my flesh. Into my bones and those places he cut free in me last night. Cuts that feel like they're bleeding now.

"Hello, *Kitten*," he says, the nickname now gross, making my skin crawl. The muscles in his arm tighten as he flexes his fingers on the weapon aimed at my father's face.

"Ah, *fuck*, Delly," Clyde hisses, like he knows, and I realize he's kneeling as well.

"Fuck." Cora breathes out the word. "No. No."

"Delilah," my father snaps, hearing the familiar way Reaper's addressing me.

My gaze drifts across the room, and I see them all standing with weapons drawn, shifting slightly as they keep the few people still in the lobby in their sights. A slice of pain cuts through my gut, making it feel like my insides are spilling onto the glossy floor, pooling with the guard's blood.

Last night flashes through my mind. Breaker's devouring kiss between my legs, Viper in my mouth, stroking my tongue with his cock. My guts churn and I lean forward, clenching my jaw as I squeeze myself tighter, trying to hold the shattered pieces in place.

Striker. I could still taste him this morning when I woke. Smell them all on my skin.

Feeling like the world is crashing around me, I drag my gaze back to Reaper.

Last night he claimed me. Took from me. Fucking *possessed* me, and now I know why.

They were planning this even as they fucked us. Even as they brought us to pleasure. They knew that when they stormed in today, everything we experienced last night would cut worse with the knowledge of their deception. They knew how vile we'd feel when we discovered that everything they did to us, everything we *allowed*—the degradation, the using—would fucking destroy us from the inside out.

A dark tendril slithers up my spine, clawing down my arms painfully.

They *planned* this. Planned to come here today and...

"You're sick," I whisper.

Cora's choked cry makes me reach for her, wrapping my arm around her waist to keep her from falling over as she quietly cries. Reaper's fingers flex on his gun, his head twitching.

"Was my cum still leaking from between your thighs when you woke this morning?" Reaper asks, a sick gleam in his eyes making them spark with fire. "Did you have a sweet ache when you moved, remembering where I'd been?"

A strangled sound slips out of my father, and Reaper's grip tightens. "Don't fucking think about it," he warns, moving his aim from my father to me.

"What do you want?" Clyde asks. His voice is low, dangerous. Murderous.

The gun aims at my chest. "Delilah," Reaper says, my name spilling from him with such hatred it makes my skin prick.

Like the single word slices the inside of his mouth, poisoning him. He nods to Cora. "This one too."

A low gravelly growl escapes Clyde, but I place a hand on his back, silently begging him to remain calm. This could all go bad quickly. Reaper and the three have already shot two guards. I know they'll have no qualms about shooting Clyde.

"How dare you come into my house!" my father screams, his entire body trembling with anger. "And try to take what belongs to me!"

A dark chuckle escapes Reaper as his eyes move back to me. He lifts his free hand and positions his glasses, shielding his eyes. Raising his arm, he motions to the three at his back and Striker moves forward, pulling black fabric from a bag strapped around his chest.

A choked sob leaves me and I bite my lip to stop the sting of tears remembering his sweet kiss. His passionate groans.

He hesitates for a millisecond, seeming to watch me for a heartbeat, but then leans forward, gripping Cora by her shoulder and pulling her away.

Her scream cuts through the room like a blade. My insides twist painfully. My grip on her tightens, but he yanks her away, and she slips from my grasp.

"Let her go!" my father shouts. The butt of Reaper's weapon hits his temple and my father falls to the side, his hand flying to the side of his face.

"Please, no!" Cora shrieks as Striker drags her to him, her legs thrashing in the guard's blood, soaking her skirt and nylons. My eyes meet hers, and I see my terror mirrored back at me.

This is my fault. I felt it in him last night. His anger. The familiar way he addressed me. Like he knew me. Because he did.

"Why are you doing this?" I ask Reaper, torn between wanting to reach for Cora and calm my father.

I know he smirks. That fucking mask he wears has smirked at me from the moment I laid eyes on him. Smirking as he fooled me. Smirking with the knowledge, I let him. When he doesn't answer, I cut my eyes to Viper and Breaker in the back of the lobby, feeling my heart crack a little more.

Tiny thing. Sweetheart.

Fucking *lies*.

My father sits upright with the help of Clyde and asks, "What do you want? Money?"

Reaper's menacing laugh makes my nipples tighten.

"I already told you," Reaper says as Striker pulls the black pillowcase over Cora's head. Her cries suddenly stop and my blood turns to ice. She *hates* the dark.

"Did he send you?" Rune asks, his voice growing husky with something I don't recognize, making my focus snap to him. "He fucking sent you, didn't he?"

Viper moves forward and grips Cora, pulling her away from Striker and to her feet, plastering her to his chest as he backs away to the exit.

"No!" Clyde screams, one arm reaching for her as he attempts to get up, but Striker aims his weapon at him.

"Don't, Mr. Harlow," he hisses.

With a single gesture from Reaper, Striker moves forward and grips my arm. Panicked dread explodes in my chest and I scramble back, my other heel slipping off. Shoving him away, I stand on my own, glaring at the dark glasses covering his eyes, hoping he can feel the hatred pouring from me.

My father's panicked expression eats at my insides as he glances from me to Clyde, then slides over to Cora gripped by Viper at the doors.

"He's doing this," my father whispers. The way his eyes fall to the floor, the way he seems to crumble, makes my knees give, but Striker keeps me up, using his muscular arm around my waist to keep me from falling. Rune's eyes move back up to Reaper. "He's come to collect."

"And I'm here for revenge," Reaper says, right before fabric covers my head and my world goes black.

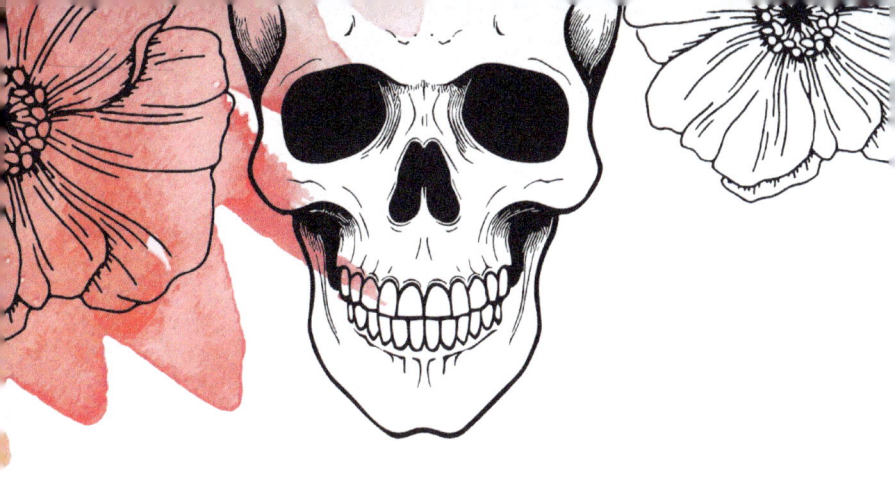

The story continues with

STRIKER

The UnMasked Series Book 2

Cast of Characters

Delilah Gavin – 26, Virgo

Cora Julian – 25, Cancer

Reaper – 35, Virgo

Striker – 30, Gemini

Breaker – 28, Taurus

Viper – 32, Sagittarius

Rune Gavin – 53, Scorpio

Clyde Harlow, 55, Gemini

Zane Devin, 40, Libra

Thank you for taking the time to read this book!

If you enjoyed, please consider leaving a review.

Reviews help readers find new books!

ABOUT THE AUTHOR

Finding Strength in Love

DARK STEAMY ROMANCE

Meet Fanny Lee Savage, the bestselling romance author known for her suspenseful and steamy stories of characters overcoming trauma and hardships. In her novels, she explores the resilience of the human spirit and the power of love to heal even the deepest wounds.

In the *Guardian Series*, a paranormal romance with a set in modern times, Ms. Savage combines her love of ancient history and folklore to create a dark new world. Her action-packed *Playhouse Series* immerses readers into the underworld of Miami and the inner workings of the modern-day mob. Her novels are full of sensual romance, dark humor, and edge of your seat suspense.

If you're looking for a romantic read that will make you laugh, cry, and fall in love, Ms. Savages' books are for you. Every story is full of sensual (steamy) romance, and characters that struggle with finding the courage to move forward and fight for themselves. With her powerful storytelling, she'll take you on an emotional journey that will stay with you long after you've turned the last page.

Also By...

Contemporary Romance

The Fake Series

Fake Hearts and Kisses

Fake Coral and Keys

Fake Whiskey and Words

Fake Enemies and Allies

Fake Lovers and Liaisons

Fake Book 6 — COMING SOON

Taboo/Forbidden Love Series—Standalone Novelettes

One Night—A Taboo Stepbrother Romance

Mr. Dylan—A Boss Romance

Romantic Suspense

The Playhouse Series

Seven Days

Four Days

Seven Weeks

Paranormal Romance (Modern Fantasy)

The Guardian Series

In the Shadow of Angels

In the Shadow of Monsters

In the Shadow of Demons – COMING SOON

Printed in Great Britain
by Amazon